CAROL DRINKWATER

THE HAUNTED
❖ SCHOOL ❖

PUFFIN BOOKS

PUFFIN BOOKS

Penguin Books Ltd, 27 Wrights Lane, London W8 5TZ (Publishing and Editorial)
and Harmondsworth, Middlesex, England (Distribution and Warehouse)
Viking Penguin Inc., 40 West 23rd Street, New York, New York 10010, USA
Penguin Books Australia Ltd, Ringwood, Victoria, Australia
Penguin Books Canada Ltd, 2801 John Street, Markham, Ontario, Canada L3R 1B4
Penguin Books (NZ) Ltd, 182–190 Wairau Road, Auckland 10, New Zealand

First published by Penguin Books Australia 1986
Published in Puffin Books in Great Britain 1987

Library of Congress catalog card number: 87–61907

Printed and bound in Great Britain by
Cox & Wyman Ltd, Reading

CIP

Drinkwater, Carol.
The haunted school.

ISBN 0 14 032150 0 (pbk.).

I. Title.

823'.914

To
Phyllis McCormack,
Michel Noll
and, of course,
to Australia.

My very special thanks to
Jean Diamond,
Julie Watts
for their constant support.

The action of *The Haunted School* takes place in New South Wales, Australia, in 1863, three years before the New South Wales Public School Act.

❖ *CHAPTER ONE* ❖

Fanny Crowe slowly opened her eyes. She lay quietly listening to the early morning sounds of young ladies making their way downstairs to breakfast. She lifted her head and peered around the spartan dormitory. It was still unoccupied, save for herself. The other five beds stood empty, neatly blanketed. They had not been slept in. It was the smallest, the most cramped room and always the last to be occupied. It lay still and bleak.

Outside in the corridor, by contrast, doors were banging and feet were clattering, as well-spoken English ladies shouted to one another: 'Wait for me, Cissie, I haven't finished making my bed!' 'You should get up earlier, lazy. I'll save you a place.'

Fanny listened to delicate shoes pounding excitedly down the stairs as she sullenly laid her head back onto the pillow. She estimated by the early morning light beaming through the window that it must be nearly seven o'clock. Normally she rose before six and was the first downstairs, busily laying the tables in the dining room. Her enthusiasm for life in the new country, though, had crept away these last two or three days. Getting out of bed, like everything else, required so much effort.

'September 14th,' thought Fanny gloomily. 'Early spring. I've been here three months!' Her thoughts drifted back to home, an indulgence she rarely allowed herself. 'It'll be late summer there now. Still warm enough for walks in the park. Probably all the leaves are turning russet and gold. Ah England!' she sighed.

Not that she disliked Sydney. Indeed not. In these last lonely months she had passsed many a warm winter's afternoon, walking by newly discovered beaches around the magnificent harbour, watching the strong white waves crash against glistening brown rocks. This was a pleasure she had never known in England. Fanny was a London-born girl who had rarely been given opportunities to walk by the coast. She had never seen such wild seas or such soft white sand, except during her voyage.

As a child when her parents were still alive, she had once been taken to the popular English resort of Brighton. It had been quite different there, she remembered, with its gentle grey summer waves politely lapping against a pebbly beach. 'This is where your mother and I passed our honeymoon weekend,' her dear father had confided to her whilst strolling one afternoon along the front. How she had gloried in watching the elegant ladies promenade along the Brighton esplanade dressed in their variously coloured crinolines and bonnets and carrying laced and frilled parasols.

'Summer in England,' she reflected longingly. She had no way of knowing anything of this last summer. Her ties with that distant island were severed now. The only news she ever received was trivial gossip from the new arrivals.

There was her aunt, of course, but somehow Fanny could not bring herself to write Aunt Alice another letter, particularly as her present circumstances were so uncertain. She had written once, as had been expected, informing her aunt that the interminable ninety-day crossing had been accomplished safely, although not entirely comfortably. She had carefully avoided disclosing in her letter the real discomforts of travelling second-class. Aunt Alice would have been appalled to learn of Fanny's cramped cabin conditions, her lack of nourishing food and the numbers of fellow passengers that her niece had witnessed fall sick during the long voyage. One, she remembered, had even died from dysentery.

Her aunt had sent a curt reply stating her disapproval about 'decent young ladies from good families leaving home and starting out on their own.' How many times had the young Fanny sat in her aunt's stately London flat and listened to Aunt Alice lecture her on the subject! Thankfully she was spared that humiliation now. She pushed back the threadbare patchwork quilt with her heels.

'What would dear Aunt Alice say if she could see me now?' She shuddered at the question and got resolutely out of her lumpy bed. 'Fanny you must stop this maudlin daydreaming at once! It serves no purpose. Get dressed and ready for your morning appointment,' she reprimanded as she poured herself some water for washing from the pink and white porcelain jug which sat on the ancient cupboard next to her bed. 'Nevertheless, facts must be faced. Something needs to be done. Indeed, with luck, something will be done today!' And she splashed the cold water over her face.

Only yesterday she had counted out her last twenty pounds. How long could that last?

'This hostel,' she thought crossly, rubbing her face dry, 'is certainly not cheap! Perhaps my first act of economy would be to find myself somewhere else to stay.' But of course the question was, as it always was when she proceeded along this particular train of thought: 'Where else could a single lady of good family live, in a city like Sydney, without compromising herself?'

The answer was always the same. Nowhere. She

could not entertain moving to a cheaper hostel and surrounding herself with domestic workers, or, worse still, ladies of ill repute. No, since she had not acquired a position which offered accommodation, she was obliged to reside in this Anglican home for well-bred English ladies or lose her reputation.

'It's inevitable,' she sighed, sitting on the edge of her bed, aimlessly untying the white bow at the neck of her crisp cotton nightgown.

Fanny calculated that, including the voyage, it was almost eight months since she had left England under the auspices of the FMCES.

'Oh, yes, the FMCES,' she muttered crossly. 'The answer to my dreams!' She folded up her nightgown and scoffed as she remembered the promises made to her by the FMCES. Like so many young governesses before her, she had been led to believe that for young ladies from good families both work and marriage prospects were far more abundant in the antipodes.

She had never considered herself unattractive, yet she had managed to reach the age of twenty-nine without a single marriage prospect, and when her father died nearly a year ago, she was left with very little money and tedious prospects for a future life. Quite by chance she had read an article in *The Times* newspaper giving a resumé of the results of the first year's work of a group calling themselves The Female Middle Class Emigration Society: *Qualified teachers and governesses are very much sought after in Australia, at salaries far exceeding anything they could be offered in England.*

'That's just what I need,' Fanny had cried out. 'A new chance at life!'

'A new chance at life, huh!' she thought now, during her morning toilet, taking stock of herself and reflecting upon that fateful day. Yet even on this bright spring morning in Sydney, she had to admit that her looks were more an advantage than otherwise. 'Even if I have just recently celebrated my thirtieth birthday.'

Fanny reached for the drawer in which she kept her stockings. Alas, the choice was no longer plentiful. She had no money for such luxuries now. Nevertheless, she took the time to consider which pair would be the most suitable for her very important morning meeting – the meeting that she had gone to such lengths to arrange.

'Nothing that would offend propriety, Fanny,' she warned herself. 'After all, she is the bishop's wife.' She had only met the lady once before, during an Anglican afternoon tea gathering for the poor and needy. She and several other young governesses had been requested to offer their services to the charity by pouring the teas. Mrs Trippery, the bishop's wife, had organised the event.

After another moment's deliberation she chose a simple black pair. The warmth of the early spring morning spoke more in favour of a lighter choice but it was important she give the right impression this morning. As she slipped the well-worn stockings over her pretty legs she giggled nervously to herself. Her present edginess reminded her of that other meeting, with her great Aunt Alice, all those months ago back in England. . .

After she had received the small inheritance left to her by her father Fanny had calculated that, with a loan from the FMCES for her passage to Australia, she would be able to set herself up in Sydney and await a suitable post as governess with a wealthy Australian family. There was, she had discovered, only one barrier. The Female Middle Class Emigration Society would not lend money or offer assistance for the passage to any of the colonies without a written guarantee from a reputable member of British society. Fanny only had one living relative – her deceased mother's wealthy spinster aunt. Alice, a finely bred, opinionated lady, whose own family had bequeathed her a tidy fortune, was considered by all who knew her to be 'very careful with her money'. Alas, Fanny had had no choice. She had to approach Great Aunt Alice.

That meeting had filled her with trepidation. On arriving at Aunt Alice's elegantly varnished door that day nearly a year ago, she had known that she was in for a battle, but one that she was wholly determined to win.

'What sort of a document is this?' her aunt had enquired, peering over her lorgnettes at the white paper that Fanny had handed to her, once the maid had left the room and afternoon tea had been ordered.

'It's a contract, Aunt Alice, guaranteeing the loan for my passage to Australia, should I fail to repay it within the allotted first thirty months.'

'Australia!' Alice dropped her glasses in horror. 'My dear niece, have you taken leave of your senses?' she had screeched at Fanny – rather inelegantly, Fanny had thought as she sat watching her aunt's lorgnettes clink against an ornate gold brooch.

Alice continued. 'I can only say that I am more than a little relieved that your poor dear mother is lying in her grave and not here to witness her only child in the throes of early insanity!'

Fanny had not been deterred by this ungracious outburst. She knew her aunt too well. It was everything she had expected. So she had stuck firmly to her guns and had cleverly led her aunt to believe that she could have been financially responsible for Fanny anyway, even in London.

'You see, dear Aunt, what if I should not prosper here? There are precious few positions in England for young governesses, even those such as myself who can teach French and music. What if I should not find employment? I could never keep up the necessary payments on the house. As you know, Father's will does not permit me to sell it. I have devoted myself these past fifteen years to Father and his needs. I have had no social life of my own and have met no eligible gentlemen. I have found no husband and, as far as I can tell, have very little prospect of obtaining one now – should that be my heart's desire, which it is not! So you see, dear Aunt, I am quite on my own. If I should fall upon hard times who would help me?'

Alice, a spinster of quite some advanced years, had been delighted to hear her niece accept that life was not necessarily about possessing a husband. That comment had gone in Fanny's favour, as Fanny had intended. When Alice had finally realised how limited Fanny's opportunities really were and that she herself could end up being responsible for her niece, she had begrudgingly lifted her fine-nibbed pen to sign the papers. . .

'What a triumph that day seemed to me, then,' Fanny reminisced now as she dressed in the hostel dormitory. Carefully stepping into her elegant taffeta frock, she hooked the tightly fitting, burgundy bodice into place and then paused to check herself in the mirror. 'Oh,' she cried. 'If only this morning's meeting were to end so successfully.'

Her stomach was beginning to rumble. She was uncertain if it was a reminder that breakfast was later than usual or if it was just plain nerves. She dreaded the prospect of pleading with the bishop's wife. She could not clearly picture the woman. Nevertheless a vague memory of Bishop Trippery's wife, presiding over teas in a large ostentatious hat, managed to heighten Fanny's nerves. She must take control of herself. She had no choice. She had to obtain help from somewhere. She certainly could not go back to London, even if she were able to raise the fare – not after those last words that Aunt Alice had spoken as she had walked triumphantly to her sitting room door: 'Take your contract, Fanny, but mind you never return here again if you should bring further disgrace upon your family – as you undoubtedly will. *Australia!'*

Fanny shuddered and began pinning up her untidy chestnut curls. Forced as she now was to plead with a lady she hardly knew, whose only connection to her was that she was the patroness of the FMCES, Fanny had to admit that things had not gone according to plan. Perhaps, though she dare not think about it, she would have to ask the bishop's wife for money. It was her last resort. She could no longer afford to consider the disgrace she may be bringing on her family. What would they have said if they had known she was a mere twenty pounds away from accepting domestic work?

She picked up the burgundy velvet purse that matched her frock and took a deep breath. She was ready to face her fate. After one final glance in her glass she made her way out of the door, along the dark, windowless corridor and down the bare wooden stairs to the hall. As always she went to the noticeboard first. Although it was still too early she crossed her fingers and quietly said a prayer. 'Please let it be today that someone has pinned up a notice requesting a governess.' She would accept any position now, even one without music. She turned away, disappointed. The board was empty, as it had been for the past several weeks, save for handwritten notes stating times of church services and requests for assistants at forthcoming 'summer fayres'.

She had not noticed the hostel matron watching her from a desk near the main doorway. The plain lady, with her dull brown hair scraped severely from her face, always offered Fanny a kind word.

'Something'll turn up soon, Miss Crowe. You see if I'm not right.'

Fanny turned quickly, attempting a smile. 'Yes, I expect so,' she replied graciously and walked despondently into the dining room.

The large room echoed with the clatter of mugs and plates. Fanny sat at a table near the window. She decided against joining any of the ladies scattered around the tables in small groups, but morosely began to eat her breakfast. She had recently taken to eating a meal of eggs and damper or some such, whether hungry or not, knowing that this saved her buying any lunch later. As she poured her tea from a large enamel pot in the middle of the room, a burst of giggling across the tables caught her attention.

Looking up, she spied a new batch of young ladies, leaning in close to one another. She recognised them as a group that had arrived several days earlier from England. As she returned to her seat with her mug of hot tea, she watched them whispering tales to one another about their voyage. She could not hear exactly what they were saying, but a pretty, roundish, fair-haired girl about eighteen years old seemed to be telling her very attentive companions the details of an intrigue that she had experienced on the ship. The wide-eyed, captured audience responded with sighs and naughty giggles. The girls' enthusiasm and vivacity left Fanny feeling disgruntled. She also noticed how much younger they seemed. At thirty, she must now be the oldest woman staying at the hostel. That sad fact would not further her chances of employment. She ate heartily, telling herself that her intended trip to the bishop's wife was a very sensible decision. There was no reason to feel nervous.

❖

Richard Blackburn woke with a start. He thought he had heard a scream. He was hot and damp, almost feverish.

'Must've been a nightmare,' he moaned as he rubbed his hand over his sticky torso. He was feeling uncomfortable with a nervous, sick sensation in the pit of his stomach. He rolled over and looked out of the window. 'Not even dawn.' He rolled back, to try and sleep again.

But something disturbed him. The sound of a cupboard banging downstairs caught his attention. He lifted his head away from the linen pillow. Someone was moving in the kitchen. He assumed by the light that it was too early even for his father. He lay for a while, trying in his drowsy state to put a picture to the sounds he was hearing. Water was being poured, then a chair grated against the stone floor, a few heavy footsteps, then nothing. Silence had descended once more in the large family kitchen at *Rosewood*.

'It *must* be father,' Richard decided. 'Who else could it be?' The slim, dark-haired boy slipped out of bed quietly. He wanted to be sure. He crept across the room, through the open door and along the landing, careful to avoid the creakiest parts of the floor, fearful of waking his sisters. As he stole down the stairs he leaned over the bannisters and peered down into the hallway. He could just make out the large, burly figure of his father sitting alone with his back to the door, a mug of tea in his hand, staring out of the window into the dimly dawning light across the valley. Richard continued to the bottom of the stairs and crept quietly towards him, nervous of disturbing him.

'Father,' he whispered, edging into the semi-dark kitchen, 'Are you all right?'

Henry Blackburn did not turn around nor did he answer his son. He just continued gazing out of the window, one hand resting his mug of tea on the sturdy cedar table, the other clenched in his lap, while Richard stood behind him conscious of the cold stone floor under his bare feet. He noticed his father was already dressed, though not in his farm clothes. He was wearing his black suit. One that Richard had seen only on the occasional Sundays when Henry had accompanied his family to chapel. His well-worn black hat lay on the table.

'Father,' Richard said, a little louder. 'It's still very early. Is there anything I can do?'

Henry remained staring out of the window. Richard longed in that moment to say something about the accident. He wanted his father to know that he understood what he was feeling, that he missed his mother, too, but he couldn't think of any words. His mouth felt dry.

'Go back to bed,' his father said eventually in his thick Scottish accent. 'I'll need you to take care of your sisters later. Get some sleep now. I'm fine here.'

Without another word, Richard crept back upstairs and crawled into bed, though like his father he could not sleep. He just lay listening to the silence in the kitchen. Suddenly he started to weep. Why was all this happening to him? Why had he lost his mother whom he'd loved so much? He hated himself for crying. 'It's a sign of weakness,' his father had always taught him. He felt so ashamed. He bit his lip tight to quieten the sobbing and eventually fell asleep.

An hour or so later he was woken by his father shaking him from his stolen sleep. 'Get out of bed, boy, and help your sisters to dress.' He opened his bleary eyes and crawled out of bed as his father disappeared from the room.

Richard dressed quickly, without washing or combing his hair, and hurried along the corridor to his sisters' room. The door was open. He took one or two reticent steps and stood uncomfortably inside the girls' untidy bedroom, impatiently waiting for Vanessa and Clarissa.

'Come on! Aren't you ready yet?' He was fed up with them. He hated being put in charge because girls were always so slow. 'Hurry up, Clarissa, and put your boots on.' He slumped back against the wall. As he did so he heard a knock downstairs at the front door. He crept out onto the creaky carpeted landing, leaving his sisters to finish dressing.

It was Reverend Dalton. The twelve-year-old boy leaned over the bannisters straining to hear the conversation. The adults were whispering in the hall below as they moved into the drawing room. It was almost impossible to catch anything of what they were saying. It was made worse by Vanessa, the older of his two sisters, who had started crying.

'Ssssh!' hissed Richard. He swung round angrily and saw her sitting on the elegant French wooden chest at the foot of her bed, an heirloom from their mother's family. She was now partially clad in her new dark grey dress although she had not, as yet, fastened the hooks. The plain robe fell loosely from her shoulders. She was blowing her nose with the hem of it and rubbing her eyes with the sleeve. Clarissa, her beautiful long blonde hair still uncombed, stood at her side, awkwardly balanced on the outer edges of her now laced-up boots. She looked ill at ease, silently watching her unhappy sister. She turned her pretty grey eyes to Richard, helplessly signalling to him to do something.

After some deliberation, he accepted her silent plea and moved back into the room towards the two girls. He placed his hand awkwardly on Vanessa's light, ringleted hair. 'Why don't you stop crying?' he said, more brusquely than compassionately. 'You know very well Father and I will look after you.'

'It's all right for you! You're a boy!' she snapped. 'I heard Father say he's going to take you with him. But what about us? It won't ever be the same for me and Clarissa. We'll have no one to play with or look after us. Why did Mother have to die? I hate her for going away!' She became more angry, getting redder in the face as she sobbed passionately.

Richard thought how ugly she looked when she cried, with her tousled hair inexpertly tied in ringlets. Her tempers always disgusted him.

'Shut up, Vanessa!' he said impatiently. 'Anyway, it's a sin to hate your parents. I'm going downstairs to Father. Reverend Dalton's here already so you'd better stay upstairs until you stop crying, and you'd better hurry up!'

'*I'm* not crying!' retorted Clarissa, defensively and a little proudly.

He ignored her and hurried from the room, relieved to get away. It made him uncomfortable to see anyone cry. He crept quietly down the stairs for the second time that morning, wanting to hear what was being said but nervous of disturbing the conversation. He stood by the French oak dresser in the hall, close to the half-open drawing room door. He could listen from there without being noticed. He pressed his cheek against the wooden door frame enabling him to peer into the room.

Reverend Dalton, dressed for the forthcoming

service, sat nervously on the piano stool. He spoke in a soft, conspiratorial manner.

'Believe me, Blackburn, it's the best for everyone. Send them to the city. At least for a few months, until you sort things out. A boarding school or such. On occasions such as this it's always wiser to send the children away. Until you find help here.'

Richard fought with himself to remain silent. 'Send us away!' he thought. What was he hearing? He didn't want to be sent away. Why was Reverend Dalton interfering? He leaned further into the room, anxious to see his father's reaction.

Henry Blackburn said nothing. Richard assumed he must be considering the suggestion. Slowly, the man lifted his head to face Dalton. He spoke with anger, coldly and decisively. 'They'll grow up here with me. There's an end to it, Dalton. One of the women in the village can cook and clean. Other than that,' Henry continued, 'things will go on as usual.'

'But surely, Blackburn, my other suggestion, a governess or . . .' Dalton interrupted.

'I'll not hear another word about it, Reverend. It was your damned encouragement that led my wife into that cursed hotel in the first place. So you can do me the favour of keeping your mouth shut now.'

Unaware of it, Richard had been gradually

18

drawn into the room. He stood by the open door, behind the head of the chaise longue, listening, relieved that his father was not sending him away. Where would they go anyway? They had no relatives in the city.

Dalton nervously tapped his fingers on the closed piano lid. He felt frustrated, defeated by Blackburn's quiet coldness. Suddenly he became aware of Richard standing in the room and said, rather too brightly and slightly edgily, 'Well now, young Richard! Where are those two pretty sisters of yours? I think we should be making a start.'

'Upstairs, sir. They're not quite ready.'

'Then why don't you ride to the chapel with me? The girls can follow with your father in his wagon, later.'

Richard ran back up the stairs. He had forgotten his cap. As he walked past his sisters' room he spied them sitting on Clarissa's bed, whispering. They looked up expectantly. Vanessa's eyes were red and puffy.

'I'm going on ahead with Reverend Dalton,' he announced. 'Father says you are to ride with him. He's waiting for you. So you'd better stop crying.' He did not wait for a reply but hurried along the landing to his own room, relieved to be getting out of the house. He ran downstairs out into the fresh morning air and joined Reverend Dalton who was waiting patiently in the wagon.

19

The two figures, both clad in black, sat silently side by side, their bodies lightly brushing one another as the swaying wagon knocked them off balance. Only the whistling whipbirds and the clip-clop-clipping of the horses' hooves resounded through the sparsely bushed valley. Neither spoke a word.

Richard stared ahead of him at the two brown beasts laboriously pulling them up the hill. He flicked a surreptitious glance at the pastor who seemed lost in his own earnest thoughts. Normally, he quite liked the funny, benign fellow. Maria, Richard's mother, used to spend a deal of time in the pastor's company. So why would he encourage Henry to send the three children away? She would never have wished such a thing.

Unable to fathom an answer the boy turned his gaze to the passing black wattle trees almost in bloom and to the mass of scribbly gums. He heard birds screeching overhead and looked towards the clear cobalt blue sky. Two sulphur-crested cockatoos dallied with one another way up on a branch in a tall eucalyptus tree. He had seen them a few days ago in the same tree. 'Must be making a nest,' he thought. The horses clipped on, up the hill.

'It's a difficult time for you, Richard, I can see that,' Dalton suddenly said, breaking their silence. 'But brooding about it won't help. You have to face up to it like a man. Your father will be needing help with your sisters. He'll be relying on you.'

'Is that why you wanted Papa to send us away?' Richard accused, rather more curtly than he had intended. He was choking with the burning lump in his throat. Such anger he felt, intermingled with his loss. He threw another glance at Dalton, but the mountain clergyman was preparing to steer his nags over the curved ridge at the head of the valley onto the yellowish dust track that led to Moogalloo. He was no skilled horseman, this pastor, and the task demanded his entire concentration. As the wagon rolled and bumped, wheeling itself to the right and up onto the road, Richard saw a flicker of accomplishment, perhaps relief, steal onto the older man's face. The beads of sweat on Dalton's temples glistened like diamonds under the shadow of his black church hat.

The boy turned his gaze back down into the valley, searching for signs of his father and sisters. They had not yet left *Rosewood*. Only a few grazing sheep dotted the panorama. He stared at the large, two-storey house, set in the basin, surrounded by its own land as far as the eye could see. It was a handsome gabled house with wide, elegant cedar verandahs painted the most delicate of greens. 'Appleblossom green' his mother had described it. It seemed to Richard now that he had always been happy there. As far back as he could remember it had been his home. Both his sisters were born there. He could not recollect a time when the house had not rung out with the sounds of his mother's infectious laughter. It would never be the same again.

He turned back to the road and the journey ahead of them, the two-mile ride to Moogalloo. Suddenly he feared what lay ahead of him. He did not think he could bear the final loss of his mother, or his father's sombre face staring angrily, uncomprehendingly ahead of him, while all of Moogalloo stood watching and praying. It would be easier to be with his friend, not his family.

'When we arrive in the village, Reverend, may I wait at Patrick's?'

'Very well, if you want to. But mind you don't delay us.'

❖

'My dear Fanny! What a surprise. Do come in.'

A shy, nervous young maid had opened the door and Fanny had been shown into a comfortable, even luxurious, drawing room adorned in velvet, where a portly lady had risen to greet her. But Fanny Crowe was not having the expected response to her request. Sitting on Mrs Trippery's plush chesterfield couch, she realised it had been foolish of her to assume that the bishop's wife would sympathise with her plight.

'Why should she?' Fanny thought, as she looked at the stout woman. 'She must have requests for help everyday. Why should she consider me any differently?'

'What are all the other young ladies in your situation doing, Fanny dear?'

'I honestly don't know,' Fanny replied politely. She still felt rather nervous. Carefully she placed her china cup on the polished oval table, her hands shaking slightly as she did so. 'I seem to be the only one left from the group who arrived on my boat. One or two married, several found themselves positions, others seemed to drift off in other directions. I am not really aware of anyone else being exactly in my position.'

'That is because, Fanny dear, they have done something about it. As you must do. You cannot sit alone in that frightful hostel feeling sorry for yourself. You must make a decision and act upon it.'

'I don't understand you. What sort of a decision? I cannot return to England, if that is what you mean. I have not begun to pay back the loan for my passage here.' Fanny – determined, headstrong, and frequently described as stubborn – realised this plump, complacent Mrs Trippery was actually reducing her to tears. She had come this far, faced this new life alone, spent many days without companionship, and never once shed a tear. Now, on this very morning which had begun so resolutely, she was close to weeping.

'Why ever did I pin my hopes on her?' she asked herself crossly, digging into her velvet purse for her lace handkerchief.

'I am not suggesting that you go home. Please don't get upset. It makes me nervous. I am merely telling you that if you have come this far, silly girl, it is no time to allow yourelf to be defeated.' Mrs Trippery, prim in her tight-fitting, surprisingly sober green crinoline, stirred her tea for the second time and placed the cup opposite Fanny's on the table. Fanny sensed the woman's agitation. 'Do you think it has always been easy for the bishop and myself? Don't you think we, too, have had our struggles? But he has taught me that there is always another path. Just find it. That is my advice to you.'

'How?' asked Fanny, completely bewildered.

'You could advertise in the newspapers, or move to Victoria, or Western Australia, or go into the bush and start your own school. That is what many of the young governesses unable to obtain permanent positions have done.'

'Start my own school? With no money! Where? How would I go about it?'

'Find somewhere in the bush, a tiny settlement where there is no existing school. Just be sure there is a Christian church. All will be well. I believe in you, Fanny. Now,' she said, preparing her large frame for the move, 'I must get ready for my luncheon. Please do let us know how you get on. Bishop Trippery and I are always delighted to know how our young ladies are faring.'

She stood up. 'We were the first, you know, to encourage the Society to send decent young ladies from England,' she announced proudly, and sailed like a ship across the drawing room to rest her plump hand on Fanny's shoulder. 'If you need anything else, please do not hesitate to write. We are always eager to help.'

With that she turned, full sail, and strode towards the door, which she opened in one generous gesture, and was gone – leaving poor Fanny alone in the ornate drawing room, more confused than when she had arrived.

❖ CHAPTER TWO ❖

It was a glorious spring morning in the tiny mountain settlement of Moogalloo. The air was clear and bright with neither cloud nor mist to muffle the living sounds of birds singing, dogs barking, cartwheels rolling and a blacksmith hammering, ringing through the dense bushland hills.

Joseph McCormack put down his hammer beside the anvil in his smithy, wiped his brow with his forearm and walked away from the burning furnace out into the warm sunlight. He stretched his arms to the side, yawned, and breathed deeply the clean, fresh smell of the eucalyptus trees. It was time to wash. He stepped up onto his verandah and called to his younger brother, Patrick, who was in the yard brushing their handsome chestnut mare.

'Pat!' His lilting Irish brogue rang out across the yard. 'I think we should be gettin' ourselves ready. It'll not be lookin' good to be late.'

He strolled over to a large wooden barrel

brimming with fresh, cool mountain water in a shady corner of the verandah. His brother walked the powerful creature past the front of their adjoining smithy's shack, on past the verandah of their humble wooden abode and tied her to a post. Joseph covered his grimy, sweating body with cold water. It felt good as it trickled and splashed down his back when he bent for a rag to rub his skin dry.

'Don't leave her there, in the strong sunlight! Take her round the back again. Where are your brains, boy?'

As the freckly, Celtic-faced fifteen-year-old obeyed, Joseph smiled and considered, not without a certain pride, how well he had done to have brought the lad up alone. 'Such a young fella of quality,' he reflected, and turned to walk in out of the heat, clean and refreshed.

'I promised we'd be first at the chapel. They'll be needin' help with the coffin,' he called back into the yard.

Once inside, Joseph clad himself in his only suit – a much under-used garment. Thoughtfully he buttoned his one good white shirt, the one he kept for 'best', as he considered the occasion. He himself had built the coffin that he and his brother, with others, were about to carry to the graveside.

'Ah, Maria! What a waste!' It was sincerely felt. He had secretly adored her, and had never understood what she had seen in Blackburn. 'And

27

the poor fools will blame that ghost!'

Patrick walked in out of the sunlight. 'Jo, Richard's here. Just arrived with the reverend. Says he doesn't want to sit with him in his parlour. Says can he wait with us until his pa gets here.'

Half an hour later the entire village, which consisted of barely more than a handful of inhabitants, was assembled at the graveside for the funeral of Maria Blackburn, wife of the richest squatter in the entire mountain area. She had been a highly regarded figure in this tiny community. Her absence would be sorely felt – more so because the cause of her death heightened that loss.

Everybody agreed that this tiny coach-stop village, called Moogalloo, was haunted. The tale of the ghost who walked the old hotel was often told. No one doubted it, although no one had actually seen the ghost. But Maria's fatal accident was the first real proof that any of the villagers had actually witnessed. Any of the villagers, that is, except Jeremiah Johnson.

Jeremiah Johnson was the only person not present on this sad, ill-fated morning. It was questionable whether the little wizened man who lived in a shack on top of a hill on the outskirts of Moogalloo really was a villager. Nobody expected to see him at the funeral. He always kept himself out of sight and hidden away from village life. He did not seem to like anyone. There was

28

no one, whenever his name was mentioned, or more likely whispered, who could really claim knowing him, even less who could understand his weird hermit ways.

Jeremiah Johnson was an old, retired gold digger who, with his deceased brother, Amos, had been the original settlers at Moogalloo in 1854. It was generally believed that the murder of his brother at the old hotel had unbalanced his mind. Some people felt sorry for him. They considered that he could never really be part of a community again. Although, in truth, he must have always been a loner, with only his brother for companionship during the years they had spent by themselves in the mountains, searching for gold. No one had ever heard him talk of a wife or family. No one, for that matter, even knew when he had first left England. 'Was it originally to seek his fortune on the goldfields?' they asked themselves. 'Or did he arrive even earlier, on one of the criminal ships?' Some believed him to be over a hundred years old! Some believed he had found his fortune, and now lived with it buried somewhere in his filthy old shack. There were many differing opinions and much speculation. The only agreed-upon fact was that no one knew the true tale of his past.

All that was known for certain was the story of the ghost – the ghost of the murdered gold miner, Jeremiah's brother Amos, that walked the old hotel in search of revenge. That terrible story hung over the village like a thunder cloud. Many believed it was the cause of the village never really prospering. Blackburn was no exception to that belief, unlike his beautiful late wife Maria, who refuted the story as superstitious nonsense. 'I do not believe the old hotel is haunted! No one has seen Amos Johnson's ghost, except him!' she used to tease, in her enchanting French accent.

'But now look,' the gossip was heard to say. 'Look what has happened to Maria. If she had paid more attention to the tale of Jeremiah's woeful past, and had not tried to disprove her husband's opinion, she would not be lying in her coffin this morning.'

And, indeed, the villagers would not be gathered at her graveside to say their heartfelt farewells.

Fanny stood in a dingy brown office in the centre of Sydney and counted out ten pounds from her purse. She cautiously handed over the money to the small bald-headed, rude-mannered man who sat behind the desk amongst piles of musty old ledgers. It was half of everything she possessed in the world.

'You are quite certain that the coach won't leave before three o'clock?' she asked for the second time, rather more loudly as if addressing a man who spoke no English. The clerk flicked Fanny a glance, pushed his glasses further onto his nose, considered her, and then returned his eyes to his desk. Fanny was exasperated. She could not help feeling that as the representative for Cobb and Co., the coaching company, he was exceedingly unco-operative. She felt a certain nagging doubt as to whether he really did know the company's timetable.

An old whiskered fellow in a dirty bush hat, who had been watching her from the corner of the office while swaying to and fro in a rather rickety old chair, spat some baccy onto the floor and answered for the clerk yet again.

'No good askin' twice, lady! It'll leave at three. It'll leave at three 'cos I'm drivin'. Though, for the life o' me, can't think what you'd want goin' up around them parts.'

The uncommunicative clerk finished writing Fanny's ticket, which he pushed across the desk as if he despised the very paper it was written on, and then turned to copying figures into a ledger from another identical ledger.

'Thank you,' said Fanny, carefully putting her precious ticket into her purse. 'I'll be waiting outside at three, then,' she announced rather haughtily and glanced at the driver, determined that he at least should understand, before she walked out of the airless little office and closed the door.

'Bit of a lady, eh? Hope she knows it's a four day journey, and a rough one,' the whiskered driver muttered, amused, as he dug out more baccy from his tattered jacket pocket.

'Moogalloo,' Fanny thought as she climbed the cobbled hills towards the hostel, stopping occasionally for breath and to enjoy the glorious views of boats busying themselves to and fro on the water. 'What a strange name for a town!' She referred to it as a town, although she had been expressly warned by the driver that there was absolutely nothing there, save for a store, a chapel, a few homesteads and some strange mountain folk.

'You are quite certain there is no school in the vicinity?' she had asked the old whiskered fellow.

'School!' he had scoffed. 'School! There ain't no school up around them parts. Them folks are all too crazed to know nothin' of learnin'. Believe in ghosts there, too.'

Fanny was satisfied. Moogalloo was to be her destination. She was a trifle concerned to discover that the population was rather sparse but she was not concerned for their lunatic beliefs! 'Sparse. A disadvantage for the school's revenue. Still, I suppose I must begin somewhere.' Of the limited choices available, Moogalloo seemed to offer

Fanny a place where she might approach the bush alone with at least a minimal chance for survival.

As she wandered through the streets of Sydney for probably the last time, she paused to stare in the window of a pretty little drapery store. She pressed her face against the glass and gazed longingly at the goods on offer. 'How splendid it would be,' she thought, 'to take one or two of those pretty materials with me. Perhaps when I have made a success of my new school I shall return, in an elegant coach, and buy them all!'

She hurried along the street. Time was moving on. She confessed to a certain sadness at leaving the city, with its grand harbour, although she had no friends there and all her days until now had been filled with concern. If she were really honest with herself she also felt a tiny sense of foreboding.

'Life in the bush! The Australian outback! Surely,' she thought, 'a lady of class and breeding is worthy of something finer than a life in the Blue Mountain outback.' Perhaps she would find it intolerable. But no other choice presented itself to her.

The final few bars of the hymn resounded through the mountains seconds after the village congregation had finished singing. Reverend Dalton spoke the last word of his service and paused for a moment. Around him could be heard muttered Amens. He crossed himself and began to move away from the grave. Respectfully, the entire village drifted away too, leaving Henry Blackburn standing alone, his head bowed low. A plump, florid-faced lady, Liza Roundway, discreetly shepherded the three Blackburn children away from the graveside and their father.

'Let 'im be for a few minutes,' she whispered to them. Richard resented her interference. But this was not the moment to complain.

Since the death of Maria Blackburn Liza Roundway had taken it upon herself to include visits to the bereaved household among her daily chores. At home, sitting on the verandah two evenings previously, she had expressed to her husband her intention to assist the family. Adam had tersely told her that she would be far better tending to her own family and keeping out of the affairs of others. 'Particularly such as the Blackburns,' he had said, 'who certainly won't thank you for the kindness.'

'And what of those poor children, Adam? You call yourself a Christian man. I'm ashamed! Wouldn't you want to see our little 'uns cared for if anything should strike me down?'

Adam seriously doubted whether anything could strike Liza down, but he kept that thought to himself. He knew that her mind was made up.

Anything he might say to warn her against meddling would only give her more confirmation that: 'It was indeed an 'eathen man that I married!' He settled for silence, as he usually did, knowing that she would follow her purpose whatever, and that his time was better spent earning the family bread.

Adam had been fond of Maria too, and had nothing against Richard or his two young sisters. 'Indeed,' he thought. 'Why should they suffer for their father's miserable cold nature?' So he resigned himself to Liza's plans. She would care for the three partially orphaned youngsters and he would say no more on the subject.

Back inside the hostel dormitory, Fanny began to pack her carpet bag, gathering together her books and carefully wrapping her few treasured possessions, including a locket that had belonged to her mother, a photograph of her parents elegantly framed in silver, and a floral scent-bag, given to her by her father. Everything that had travelled with her from London. Her clothes went back into her trunk which she lovingly locked, ready for her new journey. That very act was like a key to her.

'Fanny Crowe, you are off again. You are beginning a whole new life!'

As she carted her heavy belongings down the stairs she felt a glimmer of excitement within her. She felt again that thirst for adventure, that longing that had driven her twelve thousand miles across the world. She certainly felt no sadness, no pangs of emotion as she bid farewell to all the younger governesses who, in the safety of one of Sydney's hostels for middle-class English ladies, still awaited their destinies. Standing in the doorway the young ladies waved and shouted their fond farewells as Fanny stepped boldly out into the sunlight shining on the cobbled street.

Suddenly the spinster matron pushed herself through the chattering throng and lifted Fanny's trunk into the hansom cab that was waiting to transport her to the offices of Cobb and Co.

'You take care o' yourself, Miss Crowe. There are bushrangers, black fellows and all sorts out there. No place for a lady.' And she bustled Fanny and her carpet bag into the empty cab.

Fanny breathed a deep sigh as the driver spurred his horse into movement. She was on her way. Nothing would induce her to return now. All her hopes lay near the end of the coach line, in the tiny village named Moogalloo.

❖ CHAPTER THREE ❖

After four days of exhausting, bumpy travelling, pressed against a coachload of miners, drunks and vagrants, Fanny was finally awoken by the shouts of the old whiskered driver whipping the weary horses into a dusty mountain settlement.

'We've got 'ere, lady! This is it! Moogalloo!'

The coach pulled up outside the general store and the driver began throwing Fanny's precious luggage to the ground. She leaned over to look out of the window. Her stomach was still churning from the hideous journey. She felt weak, sick and dirty. Her elegant pale mauve travelling dress was splattered with mud.

Her attention was drawn to a small group of inquisitive children gathering around the coach. Their appearance was ragged and unkempt. She stepped from the coach onto the dusty ground and the small group of urchins retreated in awe. A lady in fine travelling clothes, albeit creased and grimy, was a rare sight to these poor scruffy children. She mustered a smile but they only stared at her in unbelieving silence. She realised she was almost incapable of moving her limbs. Her whole body seemed to have atrophied. The driver nodded her a brusque farewell and set off to the store for much-needed tucker before proceeding on his way across the rugged range, to Benningee.

Fanny looked about her. The whiskered old fellow had not lied. This Moogalloo was barely more than a sleepy hamlet boasting a mere handful of buildings and a few white goldminers' tents dotted around the surrounding hills. She scanned the village in search of the chapel. There, across the semi-deserted street, sat the smallest place of worship she had ever set eyes on.

Reverend Dalton was sitting at his parlour desk, writing, when he was disturbed by the arrival of the rolling old coach. Sometimes, when he expected a letter or parcel from Sydney, he wandered along the main street, the only street, to greet the driver. This week he did not expect any mail so he continued working, looking up only briefly to register the coach's arrival. It therefore came as quite a surprise to him when he saw a rather dishevelled yet elegant young lady struggling towards the chapel. She was carrying, or rather dragging, a considerable load. He rose and waited at the door to greet her, knowing that she could not be going anywhere but to him. After a moment he realised his ill-manners and hurried across the dusty path to assist her with her luggage.

Fanny saw the frock-coated eager fellow hurrying to her aid. She immediately dropped her carpet bag in the street and collapsed onto her trunk, wiping her brow with a lace handkerchief.

'Oh, Reverend, thank goodness!' she cried, panting. 'I'm exhausted! I can't walk another step!'

Poor Reverend Dalton, struggling with the luggage, staggered back to his tiny wooden chapel. He was a little too elderly for such exertion! He gratefully deposited Fanny's worldly possessions onto the step.

After they had both taken a moment to recover, Dalton invited the young lady into his cramped parlour.

'It's hardly a presbytery, but you are most welcome,' he said apologetically, still panting and wheezing, as Fanny collapsed into the only comfortable chair.

She introduced herself, while removing her grimy yet beautifully plumed bonnet, and proceeded to enlist the reverend's help by explaining to him the extent of her plight.

'So you see, I do not know a soul in Moogalloo,' she concluded. 'The coach driver very kindly suggested that you would undoubtedly assist me to start my school here. Just until I find my own way, of course.'

Dalton fiddled with the buttons on his coat. He was a little disconcerted. This young lady seemed very certain that he would be able to help her. However, his many years of clerical experience and his studies of composure held his amazement in check. He cleared his throat.

'I think perhaps, Miss Crowe, you have been ill-informed. There is nothing here at all. You would do far better to take the coach back a short distance and reconsider your choice of destination.'

'Oh! But I cannot, Reverend. I have no more money. I have to settle in Moogalloo. I *have* to start my school here!' Fanny cried. She was quite put out by his suggestion. It had never occurred to her that this parish might not want her little school. They did not have one. Surely, then, they needed one? Dalton was less convinced.

'We have no building for a school, Miss Crowe. Or perhaps you are intending to erect your own hall? Surely you do not think that you can conduct your classes under the shade of a tree in this hot dry land?'

Fanny was dumbfounded. It had never entered her head that there would not be a building, a pretty little school, waiting for her. She pressed her damp lace handkerchief tightly between her palms and took a deep breath. The reality was that she had nowhere else to go. How could she turn back? She knew as she sat in the tiny chapel parlour that she had to stay. There was a mere ten pounds jingling in her velvet purse.

'Dear Reverend, please think again. I realise this is a tiny bush community but surely, somewhere, there is a derelict building? Something that I could make into a home and a school? After all, the villagers must want their children to be educated?'

Finally Dalton conceded that amongst the dozen or so buildings in the village centre there was indeed the old hotel. 'But,' he added immediately, 'You could not live there. It's haunted!'

Fanny, more than a little relieved to have her prayers answered, burst out laughing. She remembered then the coach driver's description of the locals here. 'Crazy mountain folk, believe in ghosts,' he had said.

'Ha ha ha! A haunted school! That's a quaint idea. Please do show it to me. I could move in immediately. I should say, though, that I have very little money to pay my rent. I will decorate it myself, and then when I open my school I can pay back the rent. A portion of my earnings.'

Poor Reverend Dalton was completely flummoxed. 'You do not seem to understand, Miss Crowe,' he said impatiently. 'One of the dearest members of our community was buried here just the other day. She, like you, and I confess me too, had laughed at the very idea of a ghost. She had been determined to convert the old hotel into something beneficial for this community. One evening last week she foolishly went alone to the building, presumably to consider what use it could be best put to. No one knew she was there. Suddenly we all heard a heart-rending scream and ran to see what had happened. One whole side of the building had collapsed. Someone was trapped, that was all we knew. Our village carpenter, a splendid brave fellow, dared to enter the building. We, I confess, were all too afraid. It was too late, Miss Crowe. Joseph McCormack carried her into the evening light. She was already dead. You see, she had disobeyed the ghost. The ghost who promises revenge on anyone who dares to enter the building. It had sought its revenge upon her.'

He paused for a moment to allow Fanny to understand the gravity of his words, and to recover his own mounting emotion.

'Now do you see, Miss Crowe. It would be quite impossible for you to live there, and certainly inconceivable to start a school there.'

Fanny restrained a tiny giggle. 'Dear Reverend, please forgive me if I speak my mind. You are talking nonsense! You know as well as I that there are no such things as ghosts. Now, please tell me who owns the building. I would like to rent it from them.'

Reverend Dalton agreed, in his own mind, that there were no such things as ghosts. Maria

Blackburn had believed there were no such things as ghosts. 'It is a fact,' he thought. 'This young woman is right, of course.' Yet Maria Blackburn was dead. His reason told him the idea was nonsense, but his experience had shown him otherwise.

❖

'Richard!' Patrick yelled as he hurried through the bracken to join his friend who was crouching alone by the edge of the pool. 'Where've you bin? I've bin looking everywhere for you. I went to *Rosewood*, and your sisters said you'd gone to the fields with your father but later when I went to the store old Joshua Burnley said you'd bin there to buy a tin for yabbies.' The freckle-faced youth, breathless from running, sat down on a small rock at the edge of the creek, beside his friend.

'Yeah. Thought I'd do some fishing,' Richard said glumly. 'Father wanted me to work so I ran off.'

Patrick watched his friend sullenly throwing stones into the pool. He looked about him. There seemed to be no signs of fishing, no tins for crayfish.

'You all right?' he asked. Richard did not answer. Only a large golden bullfrog, partially camouflaged by surrounding flora, croaked contentedly. 'Are you upset about your ma?

Joseph says there is no ghost. Says it was an accident. Says it's obvious inside how the wall fell. The whole thing was rotten. Your ma shouldn't have been there.'

'What do you know about it?' Richard accused angrily.

'You'll be all right. You'll get used to it.'

'It's different for you. You never had a mother.'

They sat together for a while in silence. It was tough for Patrick. His friend was even less communicative than usual. He had never seen Richard so angry.

'Hey! Feel like a swim?' Normally the invitation would have excited Richard. It was the only thing he always beat his friend at. 'I'll race you!' the Irish boy challenged and he leapt to his feet, ready to tear off his clothes and dive into the cold murky water. Richard did not respond. Slowly he got up and wandered off, leaving Patrick alone to watch him slouch along the bank and disappear out of sight behind the trees.

Defeated, Patrick bent down and picked up a broken branch lying in the mud. He hurled it into the water and stood watching the circular ripples.

'Damn,' he muttered under his breath and set off, with his hands in the pockets of his scruffy knee-length breeches.

The old hotel was owned by no one! As she walked through the village with the reverend, Fanny felt elated at the prospect of seeing her new school at last, now that she had pursuaded Dalton to show her the building. She smiled shyly at the passing inhabitants, all of whom nodded deferentially to the Reverend. His earnest face and funny spindly legs made Fanny laugh. In spite of tiredness from her long journey she felt in excellent humour. 'What a pretty mountain village this is,' she thought.

'What's that tinkling sound?' she asked, as Dalton tipped his hat to a woman passing by in a scruffy bonnet and woollen shawl.

'That? Bellbirds. They're very common around these parts.'

She turned, as they walked, and faced the opposite direction to more precisely observe the surrounding hills and gaze at the stark, towering white-trunked gums reaching up towards a perfect, cloudless noon sky. 'An ideal spot to start my school and make my home,' she decided happily.

That was before she turned back and set eyes on the old hotel. As they approached the last few yards to the building, her heart plummeted. This kindly pastor had not exaggerated. The building was indeed seriously damaged and in a far sadder state of repair than she had envisaged. It was a sorry sight, entirely overgrown with ivy and weeds. The few windows that still existed had been smashed. One side wall and the entire back had crumbled and were held precariously in place by newer timbers that seemed to have been carelessly nailed up at a later date. Fanny took a step back and looked up at the roof of the building. She could just make out the lifeless words *Moogalloo Hotel* written across the timbers, which several years of hot sun and lashing rains had almost worn away. A wooden sign hanging from the verandah with the same name written on it blew aimlessly, creaking in the gentle breeze. It was an eerie sound. The building was a ghostly abandoned wreck that required far more work and financial resources than poor, disappointed Fanny had available to her.

Dalton saw the dismay in the young English woman's eyes. 'Now do you understand, Miss Crowe?' he asked gently.

She could not answer him. She could not speak for fear of her tears. Her hopes had been sorely dashed to the ground.

'Whatever shall I do, Reverend?' she said eventually. 'I had set my heart on it.'

Dalton watched her for a moment. He was a cautious man, yet a caring, compassionate soul – a solitary creature, whose closest ally had been the beautiful Maria Blackburn. During her life, Maria, a French Catholic, had been strong and vivacious.

46

He had adored her courage and outspokenness. Watching the disappointment now well up within Fanny, he thought, 'Perhaps this eccentric English woman could achieve what Maria had only dreamed of. The vision that she died for. Perhaps I and the few others who deny the existence of this wretched Johnson ghost, could assist her to build a school, to turn this cursed old building into something useful, something that Moogalloo could be proud of.'

The courage that Maria's death had temporarily taken from him was returning. 'Miss Crowe,' he said to Fanny, who was still staring forlornly at the broken-down old house, 'if it really means that much to you, if you really think that you can do it, I will help, in every way I am able. You may stay with me, in my very cramped living quarters, until this building is fit for habitation. I will tell you a secret . . . I would dearly love to see this ghost buried. Now, I suggest that you walk along this path here, and when you reach the fifth home ask for Joseph McCormack. He is our village carpenter and smithy, not a finer fellow about these parts. I think he will help you. Tell him I sent you. I'll see you later, at the chapel. I must hurry now, to finish my sermon.'

He tipped his hat and scurried back along the dusty street. Fanny watched him shuffle happily back to the chapel parlour where she had left her wordly belongings and where, thankfully, she would find a bed.

She stood alone for a moment, gazing at the disused building, listening to the breeze whistling through its cracks and timbers. Her heart was pounding with excitement.

'What a long way from England I am. Dear Aunt Alice, I have my very own haunted school!'

Ten minutes later, sitting in Joseph McCormack's ramshackle kitchen finishing her mug of tea, Fanny waited anxiously for his reply. Joseph noticed how self-consciously she had placed the tin mug on the table and how she sat uncomfortably upright on the wooden bench, her hands tightly clasped in her lap.

'Well, Miss Crowe,' he began. 'You've certainly set yourself quite a task.' He smiled at her warmly, hoping to relax her a little.

Fanny watched him lean over the simple wooden table, carved by his own hand, and pour her another mug of tea. She felt her breath. It sounded loud and rather shaky.

'Will you consider helping me, Mr McCormack? Reverend Dalton said you would. As I have explained to you already, I have no money for the time being. However, I would pay you as soon as I am able. You have my word.'

He still did not answer her. She watched him
carefully pour the milk and consider her
suggestion. She felt faintly agitated. She was not
at all used to this. Here she was, sitting alone, in
the company of a man, in his very ordinary little
cottage – a man, she could not fail to remind
herself, who in England would have been her social
inferior. It was very confusing and frustrating to
her. Why did he not answer? She could not allow
her dignity to stand in her way. She had to enlist
his help. Without it there would be no hope for
her. Normally she would have been in control. She
would have accused him of insolence. But here,
under these circumstances, she was at a loss as to
know how exactly to behave. She picked up her
mug and began sipping her second cup of tea. Her
instinct was to turn away, to look in every direction except at this carpenter. She did not allow
herself to do so. She knew her social standing and
she held her ground. Uncomfortable as it seemed,
she willed herself to meet his gaze.

Joseph, on the other hand, was quite at ease.
He was finding the encounter rather enjoyable. She
had set him a challenge that appealed to him. He
knew it was a ludicrous idea, rebuilding that
terrible old hotel and battling with the village
ghost. It would cause an outcry. That was what
attracted him to the idea. Like everyone else in

Moogalloo, he knew nothing of education and yet he felt there was certainly a place for a school. Although he had never learned to read or write, it would be a chance for Patrick. He would be proud to work for his younger brother. To give the boy an education – that would be something!

He watched her sipping her tea. 'Very ladylike,' he thought. 'The straight-laced English woman.' She reminded him a little of Maria Blackburn. She seemed just as wilful, just as determined, although the French woman had been more beautiful and serene – not like this woman who was quite uneasy with herself. 'She's very untidy,' he thought, 'for a school teacher.' In spite of her elegant clothes Fanny did sport a certain ruffled look! He liked the look of her, though.

'Well, Mr McCormack,' Fanny asked impatiently. 'What is your answer? Will you help me or not?'

He looked into her earnest, anxious face with its big brown curious eyes surrounded by wild auburn curls. Her seriousness made him want to burst out laughing. 'She is quite ridiculous, quite lovely,' he thought, 'sitting there with her English manners.'

After a moment, which to Fanny seemed an eternity, he leaned across and said to her half-whispering, half-teasing, 'Tell me, Miss Crowe, do you believe in ghosts?'

'Certainly not! They are a ridiculous notion!'

'Neither do I,' he laughed, his eyes twinkling with delight.

Suddenly Fanny felt quite affronted. This carpenter had winked at her!

❖ CHAPTER FOUR ❖

Construction work on the old hotel began the following day. The whole village was buzzing with the news. Heads peered through windows, words were whispered in Joshua Burnley's general store – always a hotbed of gossip – and conversations were snatched between labourers going about their working days. All told the same tale: 'She's takin' over the old hotel. Thinks she's goin' to learn us schooling. She'll be sorry.'

That first morning, while Fanny recovered from her exhausting journey, the two Irish brothers set off into the bush and busily chopped down gum trees. Slowly, laboriously, with the help of their chestnut mare and kindly Reverend Dalton's black horse, they lugged the wood into the village and unloaded it at the side of the wrecked building ready for the following days' strenuous work.

Fanny and Joseph, sometimes Patrick when he could be found, worked every minute of every day. Joseph sawed and hammered the new timbers for the side and rear of the building, while Fanny, who for the first few days stared horrified at the cobwebs, seemingly incapable of any manual work, eventually cleaned and scrubbed the floors and walls, and loaded and emptied wooden-wheeled barrows full of debris. She found the early spring heat quite tormenting and longed for the cool evenings. Nevertheless, she battled on determined to overcome her discomfort and to learn to accept it.

Slowly, for the first time since any of the villagers had moved to Moogalloo, the old hotel began to resemble a habitable building. Any, that is, except for Jeremiah Johnson. He remembered the hotel in its heyday. He took to passing by regularly and would pace around the building sullenly watching the work in progress. He appeared to be mourning the loss of his old hotel. Passers-by and gawping onlookers were of the opinion that he was waiting there lest his brother's ghost be disturbed and driven out. They jested, but in reality they feared the consequences of someone going against the curse. When Fanny heard the whisperings she secretly laughed at their superstition. 'Mountain folk!' she chuckled merrily to herself.

Joseph proved himself a warm and generous friend to her. She was forced to admit that she had been wrong about him. This blacksmith she had so despised at their first meeting was offering her all the assistance she needed. His enthusiasm and belief in her school was an inspiration to her.

After only five days of building Fanny's optimism was high. She collected some large discarded pieces of wood, assisted by young Patrick, dragged them to the hotel, nailed them together and painted a huge sign which she hammered to a verandah post: *School opening here shortly. All are welcome.*

Very soon all the neighbouring folk had heard the news. No one could stop the gossip. People flocked from all around the hillsides to see what no one would have believed. Some made comments, others said nothing. All had their opinion on the venture. Occasionally, as Fanny carted and carried timber and stones, breaking her nails, cutting her fingers, spoiling some of her precious English frocks, working harder than she had ever conceived possible, she overheard their remarks: 'No child 'o mine is goin' to an 'aunted school!'

Lying awake at night in her tiny room at Dalton's chapel, she would think over the mutterings and whisperings that were spreading through the village, indeed through the entire mountainside. She would lie awake tormented by the faces of villagers she had observed staring and pointing at her. Slowly it began to dawn on her what she had set herself up against. In her foolishness and desperation she had assumed that everyone would welcome her, would want her school. Now she was beginning to realise that was not true. Her task was not going to be easy.

❖

One unseasonably hot spring midday Fanny, exhausted from the heat, slumped down onto the hotel step and unwrapped the damper and fresh fruit she had just purchased from the store. Patrick sat at her side, idly loosening the laces of his heavy boots.

'Who was that dark-haired boy I saw you with earlier?' Fanny asked him, picking a crumb off the freshly made bread as they sat side by side in the shade of the verandah waiting for Joseph.

Patrick shrugged nonchalantly. 'Oh, just a friend. 's'name's Richard.' He picked up a passionfruit and tore thirstily into it.

'I've seen him several times standing by the corner of the store, watching us work,' said Fanny. 'Why don't you call him over and invite him to help us? I'd like to meet him.'

Patrick seemed loath to answer.

'I thought I heard him shouting at you this morning. Were you quarrelling?' she persisted.

'Not really,' he replied, seemingly more intent on his food than her questions. Fanny sensed something troubling him. He was rarely, in the short time she had known him, so reticent. She decided against pressing him further and began picking at her own meagre fare.

Joseph came hurrying towards them from the smithy. He was carrying a large tin bath over his shoulder, which glinted in the sunlight.

'I fixed the holes in this,' he shouted loudly, slapping the side of the tub.

Fanny broke off some bread for him as he approached, and laid it on a handkerchief beside a mug of water. Joseph set the tub down on the verandah and wiped his brow.

'You'll have a place to wash now,' he announced triumphantly.

Fanny noticed how his startling blue eyes shone with pride. They seemed brilliant against the sweat and dark grime on the cheeks and forehead of his rugged, weatherbeaten face.

'When I've got the strength to carry the water from the creek without spilling it,' she laughed. He returned her smile, untied the ragged red kerchief from around his throat, wiped his face and sat down beside his young brother.

'Have some water,' said Fanny, handing him the tin mug. He beamed at her as he leaned over to take it and downed a large gulp.

'Just as well we'll be finished here soon,' he said, satisfied, wiping his mouth with the back of his strong workman's hand. 'Days are getting too hot for this work.'

He nudged Patrick with his elbow, who sat between them, silently eating. 'Heard Richard shouting at you this morning. Angry, is he, that you're working here?'

'S'pose.'

'Understandable,' Joseph murmured, picking at the bread. 'Poor boy blames this place for his mother's death. He idolised her.'

Throughout those long, hot, hardworking days Joseph grew to be Fanny's closest ally – in truth, aside from Reverend Dalton, her only ally. He listened to her fears, soothed her doubts and taught her some of the basic rules about life in the bush. She learned to light fires, boil water in billy cans, spot the dangerous snake, collect firewood, boil up bitter apples to prevent the mosquitoes biting her fair skin, and generally prepare herself for life alone in her new bush home.

After one more week came a day of great excitement. The back room of the building had been secured and rebuilt and Fanny could now move into it. This was to be her little bedroom and sitting room. Reverend Dalton graciously gave her the simple bed she had been sleeping in, while

57

Joseph presented her with a wooden table and chair, which he had spent his evenings making for her. The room was sparsely furnished but Fanny was delighted. She declared her new quarters to be 'quite the most delightful little home I could have dreamed of.'

Alone in the evening she unpacked her leather trunk for the first time since leaving Sydney and proudly placed her few personal possessions around the room. Her one remaining bottle of English lavender water and a small silver hand mirror, an heirloom from her mother, sat proudly above the fireplace. She draped a floral shawl across the window to act as a curtain until there was time to make something more suitable. She tenderly placed all her books, including her text books, onto a shelf which Joseph had built for her. Later, he had promised, there would be another in her schoolroom, but for now the books all sat side by side. It began to look like home. In truth her new abode was very basic but Fanny didn't care. Suddenly life seemed brighter.

Fanny happily occupied her one small area and eagerly awaited the completion of the main room, the old hotel bar, which was to be her schoolroom. She now began to feel that her recent fears and misgivings had been foolishness. Why should she doubt that the village would welcome her? The two friends that she had made in Moogalloo

58

already were utterly loyal and generous. Why should the rest be different once the building was renovated and open? For the time being the villagers still regarded her with suspicion but she felt certain that when the school was ready they would be there, with their ragged youngsters eager to learn.

On the second evening alone in her new home a pot of potatoes boiled on the fire as Fanny moved contentedly about her cramped space dusting and cleaning. It came as quite a surprise to her when she was disturbed by a loud hammering at the schoolroom door. 'Who could that be?' she thought. Reverend Dalton had left her not half an hour before and both Joseph and Patrick had spent the entire day working with her, so it could not be them. Puzzled, she hurried through her future classroom and opened the door. There, standing in the semi-darkness, was Jeremiah. Fanny had never seen him so close before, so the sight of this leather-faced, shrivelled little man made her feel quite uneasy.

'S'pose folks 'ave told you who I am,' he said curtly. 'Well, I want words with you.'

'Oh, then won't you come in, Mr Jeremiah? I'm afraid I'm not quite ready to receive guests yet but you are very welcome,' she said politely as she hid the duster behind her back.

Jeremiah stepped into the half-finished schoolroom. Fanny noticed that he did not even remove his battered old hat.

'I just came to tell you, since no one else could've done, that my brother walks this place and you'd be best to pack up and go – if you value your life. You ain't wanted 'ere, and 'e won't like the idea of a school bein' run 'ere. He was a violent man and 'e didn't hold with education.'

Fanny tried hard not to show her amusement. However, the expression in Jeremiah's cold eyes soon took away her humour. She sensed his hatred and knew he meant what he said.

'Is he the ghost, your brother?'

'Aye, murdered in his sleep while I was in Sydney. A rock tumbled down on the back 'o the 'otel. I've seen 'im many times walkin' the place in the night, 'eard 'im speak too. Says 'e'll 'ave his revenge on any who come 'ere. The buildin's cursed, 'e says. None but the devil's own can live 'ere and keep safe. You'll end up like Maria Blackburn. Dead.' He stood glaring at Fanny. 'I'm warnin' you.'

She held his look, gaze for gaze. His eyes were glistening with rage. He walked to the door, opened it and turned back. 'Murdered you'll be. Mark my words.' And he disappeared into the darkness on the verandah.

In spite of herself Fanny was trembling. It was not that she believed in Jeremiah's ghost but there was something in his anger, his warning, that had frightened her. A smell of danger. She walked back into her tiny living room, placed her duster on the bed, took the boiling water off the fire and sat down. She wrapped her arms around her waist and held her stomach tight.

'Tomorrow I must introduce myself to the villagers. I have neglected them and the sooner I open my school the better for us all. I'll bury that ghost once and for all. I'll prove that it's just a figment of that old man's imagination.'

As she bent to unlace her boots, the thoughts resounding through her head sounded just a tiny bit hollow.

❖

'He is the wealthiest squatter in the district, that's true Fanny,' Joseph admitted as he guided her up the steep incline behind the school, from where she would be able to find her own way. 'But there's not a colder man about these parts,' he warned.

'But, Joseph,' Fanny argued determinedly, 'his children need someone now and I need pupils. So that is where I shall begin. I'm not afraid of him. Why should I be?'

And so Fanny, unwilling to listen to Joseph's misgivings, made her way along the hill path. Spurred on by the previous night's threats from

Jeremiah, she strode alone up the steep bush path that led the two miles around the hillside to the *Rosewood* valley. As she clambered through the thickets Joseph's words echoed in her mind. 'He can certainly afford to pay handsomely for the education and it would be an example to everyone around,' he had conceded. Her optimism ran high as she energetically climbed the hill. The three Blackburn children would be her first pupils, of that she was determined.

After walking for twenty minutes she arrived at the handpainted wooden signpost, *To Rosewood*, and she turned off the hill stepping onto a dust track. From that height she stood and looked down into the valley where she spied the elegant mansion, nestling amongst the colourful Christmas bushes and pink wedding bushes in full, early November bloom.

'It is indeed a magnificent sight,' she sighed, and paused for a moment to compose herself after the hot dusty walk before hurrying on down into the valley to make her way to the house and introduce herself.

The long pathway to the house was every bit as imposing as she had imagined it to be. The surrounding land was more cultivated than she had seen in the bush around Moogalloo itself. She approached the main front driveway from a side slip-path. A multitude of cartwheel tracks marked the rutted path under her feet and spoke evidence of the comings and goings of visitors and labourers. Startlingly electric-purple bushes swayed gently in the welcoming breeze. She had never seen such flowers before. She stood to gaze upon them, and the drooping elegance of the golden yellow wattles, to watch the visiting butterflies and birds in flight overhead.

Suddenly this abundant stillness unnerved her. Her heart began to race as she stood for a moment, hands pressed against her cream satin blouse, to catch her breath. She needed to reassure herself of the purpose of this visit. She understood why the villagers would consider this man as distant and remote. There was something chilling in the air.

But Fanny was determined to guarantee herself at least ten children for the first day of school. The list she had written of families to visit was considerable and would mean walking quite some distances between homes. If she could begin every meeting, after this one, announcing that the Blackburn children were to be amongst her first pupils, other parents would be encouraged. Their superstition would be diminished if they felt Blackburn supported her enterprise.

'And so he shall,' she promised herself as she stepped resolutely forward the last few yards that curved and led to the imposing balconied door.

She approached with a beating heart, and knocked positively on the glass.

She assumed that, although it was almost eleven o'clock, Blackburn would be home. But it was Richard who came to the door.

'He's not here. He's gone to the fields, visiting, overseeing the lambing.'

'Will he be gone all day?' Fanny enquired kindly of the boy.

He seemed reticent, suspicious. 'Probably.'

'I see.' She considered him for a moment. 'I believe you are Patrick McCormack's friend. He told me all about you. I came to invite you to my new school. Patrick will be coming.' Richard stared silently up at her, making her feel uncomfortable. 'I understand you have two younger sisters. May I say hello to them?' Fanny continued, smiling encouragingly.

After the briefest moment of hesitation Richard called to the two girls. At the same time, Fanny glanced towards the window. She thought she saw a hand let go of a lace curtain. It fell quickly into place. Was someone watching her? Someone not wanting to be seen? For a fleeting moment it crossed her mind that perhaps Henry Blackburn had not gone to the fields after all.

The two small girls arrived almost immediately and the thought slipped away. They approached tentatively, dressed identically in pale blue muslin summer frocks and white stockings, certainly the smartest children she had seen since her arrival in Moogalloo. 'They must have been listening in hallway,' she thought. The idea amused her. It was childlike. She hoped that, in spite of the boy's response, it expressed their curiosity.

Fanny crouched down to them, introduced herself and asked their names. Both answered quietly, almost inaudibly, in unison. Fanny laughed.

'And my name is Miss Crowe. I am the new teacher here in Moogalloo. I've walked over here to invite you to my school. Will you come?' The girls stood gazing at her, swaying slightly, too shy to speak. 'I believe you speak French. So do I. *Comment allez vous*?'

'Father says we're to have nothing to do with you,' interrupted Richard gruffly. Fanny lifted her head to face him, he being taller than his two sisters.

'And why is that, Richard? May I ask?'

'He says you're dangerous.'

Fanny rose from her squatting position. 'I am . . . dangerous!'

Richard was not to be deterred. 'Our mother was killed at that old hotel and Father forbids us to go there anymore. Besides, he says we don't need your English education. He'll teach us everything we need to live here on our land.'

'I see,' said Fanny. This was quite unexpected. This young boy was Patrick's friend. Although she had seen him shouting at Patrick it had never crossed her mind that she would find him as cold and closed as his father was known to be. 'And you, Richard? What about you? Do you think I'm dangerous?'

He paused, confused. She was asking him what *he* thought. He had spoken what his father had taught him.

'It's not up to me. It's up to Father,' he returned, icily. 'And I don't think you should come here any more.' With that he put his arms protectively around his sisters and shepherded them inside.

Fanny stood at the door, helplessly watching them retreat, unable to detain them longer. Just as they were disappearing into the cool, dark, elegant hallway, Vanessa shyly turned back to Fanny and gave her a tentative, almost imperceptible, smile. Then all three were shut from her, leaving her to make her way, disappointed, back up along the hillside.

Fanny's sense of despair as she set off again was quite overwhelming. She felt puzzled and shocked by what Richard had repeated to her. Why should Blackburn consider her dangerous? She could not fathom this reaction. She hurried on a few steps trying to shrug off her concern. She still had the other families to visit and the day was getting hotter. She must not dawdle, and yet this meeting nagged at her. Why should Blackburn's response be so important to her? Was it because he was wealthy and influential?

'It is because, Fanny,' she reminded herself as she wiped her brow, 'if, in spite of the accident, his children were to lead the way, no one else would fear this ridiculous ghost.' She paused for a moment, panting, and dug down into her little velvet purse to find the list she had scribbled so resolutely during her breakfast. 'I won't be beaten by him!' she muttered defiantly, as she rummaged through the bag. 'I will confront him directly. Surely once we meet, he will see I am not dangerous. Then he will have no reason to refuse me. Ridiculous notion!' She was much cheered by her logic, unfolded her list and read the next name. 'Webster. One daughter. Elsie.'

She picked up her burgundy skirt and heavy petticoats, tucked the list into her belt and set off once more, walking briskly up the steep path back to the village. It was two miles to the next family. She would have to hurry. Time was pressing on.

That same evening plump Liza Roundway busied herself with domestic chores. Adam had not yet returned from minding Blackburn's sheep. Liza's two sons were playing raucously outside in the yard. Liza moved about their simple wooden cottage busying herself with supper while deciding what she was going to say if Adam should mention his idea again.

'I met that new schoolteacher this mornin',' he had said during lunch. 'Wants the boys to take lessons with 'er. Says they'd go week Monday. I told 'er it'd be fine.' Liza had been quite taken aback, but said nothing. She kept her counsel and decided to think on it. She did not want to get Adam heated about it. Not that he ever got really heated about anything.

Liza had passed the afternoon wondering why Adam should want them to attend school, especially at the old hotel. Couldn't they learn all they wanted without lessons? Hadn't she and Adam made a life together – a humble one but nevertheless Christian – without the need of lessons? She had spied Fanny earlier in the day. While cleaning at the Blackburn home she had heard the children talking to someone at the door. She had lifted the curtain to see the new schoolteacher there. Her opinion was that she looked a stuck-up sort of creature. What need had they for her sort in the village?

She had also strolled past the old hotel earlier in the afternoon, wanting to see exactly what they were up to. She'd paid a visit to the general store as a pretext, then stood outside, quietly watching. She had seen Joseph and Patrick setting a few rafters on the roof, and old Jeremiah prowling about, snarling. She didn't like him. He made her shiver. She had to confess the old place was looking cleaner, quite transformed. But it made no difference. They were wasting their time. No one would go to school. Least of all her family. Her mind was made up. She would tell Adam as soon as he arrived home. She forbade risking the boys' lives in that cursed place for the sake of a bit of education. 'Paltry education, at that!' she thought, scalding her tongue on the burning soup.

As she approved the broth the sound of the door latch broke her train of thought. It was Adam. He said nothing, just made his way to the water jug, took off his torn shirt and stood silently washing himself. 'Lookin' tired and worn out,' Liza observed, silently. Living was not easy for them here in the mountains. 'No better than England,' she concluded, not without a certain bitterness.

She remained at the stove, stirring the soup, watching her husband out of the corner of her eye. Still neither of them spoke, for no other reason than their own thoughts and actions were more consuming. When she judged both her husband and the supper to be ready she walked over to the door and called to her sons in the yard.

'No more nonsense now. Come in and sit

yourselves.' Without waiting for their response she returned to the business of filling the bowls.

'Bread's warm,' Adam said, breaking himself a chunk. 'Freshly made, is it?'

'Aye, and the soup,' she replied, carrying the dishes to and fro.

The two pale skinny sons were transformed from lively creatures screaming and tearing around the yard like pigmy possums into silent mice. Both ate without a whisper, yet ravenously tearing at their food.

'Mind your manners, young Tom,' said their mother, moving away from the kitchen area to settle herself with her family and her food. This was their one communal meal, already well under way without her. Meals were eaten as soon as plates appeared on the table. No formalities, no Grace here, except Sundays. Just the plain, simple business of each family member feeding himself. Conversations were non-existent save for requests for another dish. When their basic, frugal meal was over, each continued with his own pursuits.

On this particular evening, after the rabbit soup and damper, the boys returned to the yard. Adam sat comfortably in his wooden rocking chair by the fire. In spite of the approaching summer, the evening mountain air occasionally forced these village folk to warm their wooden homes with roaring fires. He stared silently into the flames as he filled his clay pipe. Then he lit it and took a deep satisfied draw on it. Liza clattered back and forth with dirty dishes.

'That young school mistress was 'anging about Blackburns earlier.'

'Oh, aye.'

'Looked a proper English miss. The three children there didn't seem to take to 'er. Turned 'er away, quick as a flash. Far as I could tell. Blackburn'd told 'em to, an' all.'

Adam stared down into the flickering colours and puffed on his pipe.

'Don't know why you waste your time walkin' all that way. I told you before Blackburn'll not thank yer for yer trouble. Better 'ere you are, mindin' our business.' He fell silent, cogitating and puffing his pipe.

Liza turned from the stove to face him.

'I'll not 'ave our two attendin' that old 'otel, Adam. Maria's dead. That's witness enough to the evil waitin' in that place. No good'll come of that woman there. Not unless she's a witch. And what 'ave we to do with education? I'll keep the boys 'ere with me, 'til they're an age for workin'. Readin' and writin'. It gets you nowhere.'

'But I see no diff'rence readin' and writin' than mixin' with the Blackburns. I thought it might suit yer, thought the boys might get some benefit.'

'Aye, and what good will that do 'em? Give 'em

fancy ideas. End up in Sydney! No they'll stay 'ere.'
She took a deep breath and returned to her dishes.
There was a silence between them. Both lost again
in their separate worlds.

'If that's what you want, Liza, so be it,' Adam
conceded.

Liza, sensing him settled, moved to the opposite
side of the fire. She picked up her sewing, her
family's repairs, satisfied. She knew he was
defeated. Her point had been made. She picked
at the torn shirt, prodding it deftly with her needle.

'Daft to call 'er a witch, though,' Adam puffed
contentedly.

❖ CHAPTER FIVE ❖

It was Monday morning, the first day of Fanny's school. After five weeks, the morning she had been waiting and working for had finally arrived. She finished making her bed, took the billy off the fire and walked through the adjoining door into her smart new schoolroom. She was feeling both nervous and excited. She paused for a moment at the door to proudly survey the room. It was indeed quite a transformation. No longer was it an acrid-smelling, disused bar filled with broken bottles, rats, spiders, rotting floorboards and weeds. Now she saw before her a tidy schoolroom smelling of wood and paper and polish. Roughly hewn wooden desks nailed together from discarded boxes filled what had been the bar room, textbooks tidily stood in rows on shelves that had originally housed cobwebbed bottles, and her own lovingly prepared first day's lessons waited on her bar-counter desk.

'Mrs Trippery would be proud,' she thought with a flush of excitement, 'to see me this morning.

And what of Aunt Alice?' She had not spared a thought for Aunt Alice these past long weeks. She would write tonight, telling of her good fortune. 'How could she chastise me? She would be proud to see my determination, to know I have my very own little school. And today is the grand opening!' She had no idea who would attend. She hardly dared hope the classroom would be full, although the school was now well known within the community and the surrounding areas. The kindly Reverend Dalton had even announced it at chapel these past two Sundays.

For a moment she moved around the desks and benches busying herself with last minute tidying. When she could think of no more tasks to fill the time, she sat down at her desk to anxiously await her first pupils. She felt she needed a few minutes to quieten her thumping heart. She passed this time deciding who she thought would be amongst the first to arrive.

Richard Blackburn? Perhaps he would have softened his father's heart. She pictured the young boy arriving with his sisters. How warmly she would greet them! She briefly chastised herself for failing to return and see Blackburn himself. She confessed the encounter with his offspring had made her a little wary. Joseph had eased her nagging doubt by telling her that if Blackburn were intending to relent he would do so only of his own accord. 'Nothing you do or say will make the difference, Fanny, rest assured.' This had eased her guilt a little, allowing her to push the niggling concern to the back of her mind.

Several days later, when she had worried again, Joseph eased her conscience once more. 'Nobody sways his mind, Fanny. His decisions are based upon his own nature. And a cold one it is. Comes from a wealthy Scottish family. Owns most of the surrounding area, employs many of the locals but, far as I can tell, is close to no one. Too withdrawn. Worse since Maria was killed. Adored her, he did. She was the only one who could reason with him, or understand him. They built that big house between them, more than eight years ago, when I first came here. I believe he cares for those youngsters, in his way, but you'd best leave him to see sense for himself. He'll come round to you in his own time. Not one to trust others, particularly strangers. Not fond of the English either.'

That had finally decided Fanny. She would spend her time preparing her school and visiting families further afield in the surrounding valley areas. She would leave the Blackburns to fate. And the locals, still wary of her, would hear of the school at chapel.

'Dear Joseph,' Fanny thought, cupping her face in her hands, her heart still pounding expectantly.

'What would I have done without him?' As she posed this question the latch lifted on the door. She sprung from her stool, unable to contain her excitement.

'Oh, Patrick. It's you.' Her voice fell. 'I thought perhaps you were a pupil,' she added, not bothering to conceal her disappointment.

'But Fanny, I am a pupil. I promised I would be your first pupil. And here I am. Would you like me to sit down or shall I stand until some of the others arrive?' The Irish boy stepped roguishly into the schoolroom and leaned casually against Fanny's desk.

'Certainly not!' said Fanny, a little shocked. 'We are not building now. You must sit in your place. And you must call me Miss Crowe. And Patrick, it is not necessary to wear a cap in the classroom.'

A little taken aback, Patrick slid the cap from his head and walked towards the pupils' benches. Was it really only yesterday he and Fanny had giggled helplessly as she had tried to lift the desks, insisting she could manage without his help?

'Er . . . Fanny, sorry Fanny, I mean Miss Crowe . . . Is there anywhere special you would like me to sit?'

'Patrick, you must take this seriously. You may sit wherever you wish, but remember which desk it is because that will be your place every day.'

Patrick sat down in the nearest seat. He rubbed

his hand through his hair and stared self-consciously out of the window, not daring to face Fanny again. He longed desperately for the others to arrive. He had never been to school and had not the faintest idea how he should behave. For one thing it had never occurred to him that Fanny would expect him to call her Miss Crowe. 'I hope Richard comes,' he thought, gazing out of the window. His eyes wandered along the main street. Save for the occasional cart or workman going about his day no one passed.

In the large room there was an uneasy silence. Teacher and pupil sat together, neither daring to face the other nor to accept the uncomfortable truth that was gradually dawning. No one else was coming to school.

That same evening Vanessa and Clarissa walked down into the lower valley towards the fields where their father and brother had spent the day working. They passed Adam Roundway leading a carthorse back towards the stables. He nodded to them and walked slowly back towards *Rosewood*. The end of another tiring day. Blackburn had ordered an area of forest to be felled to accommodate his ever-increasing stock. It was lambing time, too. So as the girls strolled in the evening sun, weary labourers – some carrying tools, others idly smoking, some solitary and silent, others in groups chatting and cajoling – passed by them.

The men were weary from over-exertion and the girls were listless from boredom. Since their mother's death, a few weeks past, they had both been left very much alone. Occasionally they had found little tasks in the house, after breakfast had been cleared, but these did not amuse or interest them. Besides, Liza Roundway had let it be known that if she were taking the trouble to walk over to their house she preferred to run things her own way. Each day it became clearer that Henry's private grief and his work responsibilities left him no time for his daughters. Each evening they eagerly awaited his return only to be disappointed when soon after supper he would disappear to his study and bury himself in more work.

On this particular evening when the lavender-blue jacarandas and the sweet-smelling honeysuckle were in bloom, the bellbirds were singing and parakeets screeching, they strolled idly among the dusty pathways. Occasionally they paused to pick a leaf to use as a mattress for some tiny beetle or unknown insect which they would then hold steady and study with earnest intensity.

'Clarissa,' Vanessa said, as they both stooped

towards the earth, concentrating hard on a newly discovered reptile.

'Mmm,' said her younger sister, partially squirming, partially mesmerised by the wiggling creature in front of her.

'Tomorrow morning I'm going to see Miss Crowe. Will you come with me?'

Clarissa dropped the stick she had been using to poke the lizard. She slowly straightened her body, allowing it to express her extreme surprise. Could Vanessa contemplate disobeying their father's firmly laid down rule?

'You know very well what Father said. She's awful! And she's living with the ghost that killed mother. You can't go.'

'Listen to me, Clarissa.' Vanessa adopted a tone of adult sincerity. 'I don't care what Father said.' This statement raised a look of horror on her pretty young sister's face. 'I want to talk to her,' the older girl confided. Her sister only continued staring in horror. Headstrong, tempestuous Vanessa plucked up her courage and continued with the passion of one who has been hiding something. 'Clarissa, I want to go to school. I'm fed up! I want to learn new things. I don't believe Mother would have forbidden us. She taught us. She went there! I bet she'd've loved us to go to school.'

She paused, much relieved at having finally

spoken her mind. Clarissa, the more placid and obedient of the two, stared into her sister's intent face and felt a large tear roll down her own.

'I'm not going. I won't disobey Father. Oh please don't go, Vanessa. You'll make him even more cross than he already is.'

'Then I'll go by myself. I've thought about it, and I'm going after breakfast in the morning, when Father's gone to work with Richard. I'm going to ask her to help me with my French and my reading. I'm going to ask her to beg Father, to implore him to let us go to school. Why shouldn't we go? It's not her fault Mother's dead.' Vanessa walked on, leaving her younger sister staring at her diminishing silhouette.

Clarissa was troubled. Hadn't they always been inseparable? Would she really let Vanessa go without her? If Vanessa went to school all day what would she do? Was she not lonely enough already? Perhaps if Father never found out there would be no harm in talking to Miss Crowe. In her blind bewilderment, Clarissa could see no alternative. 'If I don't like her, if she really is wicked, then I won't ever see her again,' she reasoned.

'Vanessa, Vanessa! Wait! I will come with you. On one condition. Promise we keep it a secret, even from Richard. He'll tell.'

Vanessa turned back to her sister. 'Of course, silly!'

As she spoke she saw Clarissa wave frantically. She turned to spot the familiar image of their father and brother returning home in the wagon. Both girls ran enthusiastically in its direction. The day was over. They were happy at the prospect of the family spending the evening together.

❖

Joseph tapped gently on the lit windowpane and stood quietly waiting for his knock to be answered. It was some moments before Fanny came to the door. Joseph used this time to rearrange the rough bunch of flowers which had drooped in his strong hand and to push his untidy, blond hair away from his clean shirt collar. Finally Fanny answered. Joseph thought he could see the remnants of tears in her lovely tawny brown eyes. He handed her the eucalyptus leaves, crimson bottlebrushes, sprigs of pine, bush flowers picked earlier in the evening, enjoying as he did so the abundant scents passing between them.

'I brought you these. I collected them up along the hillside where we walked the other Sunday afternoon. I thought the colours might cheer up your schoolroom.'

'Schoolroom!' wailed Fanny. 'I have no school. I'm shutting it down!' She went back inside, leaving Joseph to make his own way in.

'Fanny Crowe, I'll have none of this. D'ye hear? A strong, brave woman like you, upsetting yourself for no reason. You do indeed have a school, a smart new school. And you have your first pupil too. Or are you just too grand and uppity to count young Pat?'

'Oh no! Of course not! It's just that I expected more than one pupil. I feared some might not come yet, but Joseph, *nobody*. Not one of them!'

'So it's a tougher battle than you expected.' He noticed Fanny idly throw her flowers on the desk. 'Did I spend my days carrying wood to help you rebuild this blessed place only to have you give up at the first crossroads? Where's your spirit, Fanny?' Fanny bowed her head. She felt ashamed, knowing this rough carpenter was right. 'Listen here, young lady,' he said, moving towards her. 'I want my brother to read and write, learn things I never had a chance to learn. There's your reason for opening your school. For the rest we'll fight. And fight we will, Fanny. You know I'm with you. Now put the flowers in water and get some sleep. Patrick will be here bright and early tomorrow for his lessons and he'll expect you here, too. So will I, Fanny.'

He walked to the door and turning back to her he grinned his broad, disarming smile and said, 'Good night, Miss Crowe!'

Fanny went through to her bedroom but she did

not immediately follow Joseph's advice. She did put her flowers in water and lovingly placed them on her desk in the schoolroom. But after getting ready for bed she found she could not sleep. So she sat on the bed, feet curled up under her long nightdress, trying to read *Moby Dick* by the soft light of her bedside kerosene lamp. Nothing moved save the silent fluttering of a moth attracted by the light and soon she began to feel drowsy.

Suddenly she was shaken by the sounds of glass shattering and something heavy thudding onto the floor. Barefoot she rushed to the empty, darkened schoolroom and saw, in the moonlight, Joseph's flowers lying in a pool of their own water and splintered glass on the floor close to the desk. Almost beside them was a stone which clearly had been thrown through the window. Stepping fearfully towards the wet mess, she stooped to gather together her bruised, sodden flowers. As she did, she noticed that the stone was wrapped in a yellowing, wrinkled piece of paper. She hastily smoothed it out. Something, which she was unable to decipher in the dark, was scribbled on it. She carried the damp message to her lamp still burning in the bedroom next door and, with trembling hands, unravelled the words: *Leave now . . . You are on dangerous ground . . . A Well-Wisher!*

'A well-wisher indeed! *Somebody* in Moogalloo can write!' Fanny angrily crumpled the scribbled message and threw it into the fire. She walked determinedly back into the schoolroom, picked up a rag from beside the blackboard to mop up the water, and tenderly carried her now treasured flowers through to her room. The broken glass, she decided, could wait until the morning. Now very ready for sleep, she folded back her crocheted cover and slipped inside the welcoming bed. It had been a long day. As she lifted her hand to turn down the lamp she glanced at the flowers. They were standing in the water, elegant once again. She paused before touching the lamp and whispered a promise: 'Yes, Joseph. For the rest we'll fight.' With that she extinguished the light and put her troubled thoughts to sleep.

CHAPTER SIX

Fanny walked quickly, purposefully along the rutted dusty tracks. She had no time to lose. If she were not back by nine o'clock for the beginning of school both Joseph and Patrick would assume she really had given up. Perhaps there may even be more pupils waiting for her, although she forbade herself the luxury of indulging that heady prospect. The two Blackburn girls hurried on ahead of her, running more than walking, desperate to lead her to their father. They glanced back at her, making sure she was still following. She saw their anxious, pretty faces as they led the way, no longer hand in hand.

Earlier that morning, soon after seven, Fanny had found the girls waiting for her on the verandah. 'Please ask Father to let us come to your school,' Vanessa had begged.

Fanny had immediately put down her bucket and told them to lead the way. How could she, in spite of Joseph's warning, refuse their heartfelt request? 'We must hurry, though,' she had warned.

'I must be back to open my school!'

The sun was still climbing, and Fanny realised how physically unprepared she was for this strenuous bush life. Finally she reached the top of the ridge and staring down into a vast valley below her she spied Blackburn's wagon, standing empty and unattended. Then further over in the field she saw the man himself. He was moving slowly amongst his labourers and sheep. In the distance his young son Richard paced out the same ritual. The two girls, who had paused for a moment to catch their breath, came puffing to a standstill, one either side of her.

'There he is!' cried Vanessa, still panting.

'Right, young ladies, off we go!' And with that Fanny strode on ahead like an amazon, down the hillside towards the unsuspecting Blackburn who continued working, unaware of the approaching trio. 'God help me,' she whispered to herself, suddenly terrified to face this man at last. The two girls became slightly more reticent about keeping abreast of Fanny now.

'Mr Blackburn!' Fanny called out bravely whilst still walking. The name echoed through the valley, mingling with the constant bleating of sheep which had forced her to shout. Various labourers paused for a moment to regard the approaching group. They took the opportunity to rest a moment, then, disinterested, continued with their work. Several of those closer to her recognised her. They were less willing to turn away and resume their duties. Glances passed between them, and silently they telegraphed their interest, enjoying the knowledge that trouble could be brewing.

Fanny began waving her white lace handkerchief, which she had been using to dry her hot damp face. It was a small vestige of her distant past. Hearing his name, Henry turned to look up the hill. He took off his large black hat to wipe his brow with his sleeve. Fanny saw him register her arrival. He placed the hat slowly back onto his head and after a moment's deliberation took one or two steps in her direction.

'Mr Blackburn.' Fanny stood level with him now.

'Miss Crowe. The schoolteacher, I believe.'

She noted the sarcasm in his Scottish voice and chose to ignore it. She stared into his face, with its pallid complexion and slate grey eyes.

'As you can see, Mr Blackburn, your daughters are with me. We are here to persuade you to allow them to come to school. I know what you have told them and what you believe. However, they do seem to be interested in learning. Now that your wife has died . . .' Fanny paused for a brief moment. She did not wish to appear unsympathetic to the man's feelings. 'Now that Maria has gone, Mr Blackburn, surely you must see that it is very difficult for these two girls. You are off all day with Richard and they, poor things, are left on their own . . .'

'They are not on their own. Liza Roundway, a much respected woman in the village, has very kindly offered to give my two daughters an hour or two of her time each day.'

Fanny felt her eagerness dulled. The passion of her argument was stung by the very tone of his voice. Joseph had been right when he had said, 'It is indeed a cold nature, Fanny.' She remembered the Irishman's warning. She knew Blackburn would cut her down whatever argument she gave him.

'Mr Blackburn, please give me a chance. I know that Mrs Roundway looks after them. But she is a woman of no education. Their mother, your wife, I understand, was a woman of fine sensibilities. Surely you don't want these two girls to lose touch with all that Maria taught them? When we three chatted this morning Vanessa told me some of the things they have learned from their mother, stories she told them. I think their knowledge is quite advanced. I beg you, not for my sake or my school, but for these girls. Please do not refuse them their chance to grow into fine well-bred young women.'

Fanny waited for a response. He said nothing, only glowered at her and turned to the girls. They were both standing slightly behind Fanny almost requesting protection from her long skirt.

'Mr Blackburn, I am qualified in both music and French. Nothing these girls have been taught until now need be wasted.' She could think of nothing more to say. Her courage began to drain from her.

'Go back to the house, you two. I'll talk to you later.' The Scottish accent was thick and commanding. The two frightened young girls turned and ran back up the hill. They feared their action would reap its punishment. 'Richard!' Blackburn snapped. The boy working with the newly born lambs obeyed instantly.

'Father?' he said, running to the man's side.

'I want you to tell me if you ever catch your sisters in the presence of this woman, or if she ever dares to visit our home. Do you understand?'

'Yes, Father.'

Fanny was incensed.

'You are a cruel, cold-hearted man, Mr Blackburn. You have no right to allow your private hurt and prejudices to stand in the way of their chance at life. And you have no right to encourage this boy to spy and tell tales.'

Richard, who had moved back towards his lambs, turned to listen.

'What makes you think, Miss Crowe, that you are capable of giving them anything better? You, with your English morality and stuck-up ways. It has nothing to do with us here. Go back to where you came from and preach there! If you can survive in that building where my wife was murdered, you too must be evil.' With that he turned and walked away from Fanny. Richard discreetly moved from his father's view, though he longed to stay, to hear this woman who spoke so boldly, so bravely to his father.

'Mr Blackburn,' she called. 'You are allowing your confused, superstitious beliefs to stand in your way. More importantly, you are allowing those beliefs to prejudice your children. You have no right to do that . . . All right, I am English. My morality is perhaps different. I don't think so. But it's all I've got and I will fight you. Believe me, Mr Blackburn, you are wrong.'

Fanny, her face stinging with anger, turned and ran up the hill, her heart pounding with such extremes of emotion that she no longer knew what she had done. Would he hear what she had said, or had she merely helped his adamant resistance become more deeply entrenched? As she paused for breath on the brow of the hill, she turned once more to look back down into the valley. Blackburn, who had been watching her, quickly turned away and walked briskly back to his labourers. Fanny took a deep breath and set off down the other side of the hill.

Patrick! She had forgotten Patrick! She could

not be late for him. Nor did she intend to be. It was time to open her school.

Patrick was waiting for her on the verandah. At his side was a tiny blonde-haired girl. He stood up as Fanny, hot and bedraggled, came hurrying towards him.

'Sorry I'm late!' she called.

'I brought you another pupil, Fanny. Her name is Mary Rowe. She lives a little way from the village so she can't come every day but she'll be here when she can. Won't you, Mary?'

Fanny beamed at the shy, angelic little girl who stood in tattered clothes, no longer her size, staring back at her.

'Hello Mary, welcome to school.'

Mary squirmed with embarrassment and picked her nose.

That same afternoon Vanessa walked again from *Rosewood* to Moogalloo. She was not to be deterred. She had waited until Liza had left the house and then had set off on her own. On reaching the village, she stepped up onto Fanny's verandah and knocked cautiously on the school-room door. As she waited for Fanny to answer, praying that she was inside, Vanessa looked about her. It was still very hot and the village was deserted.

'Vanessa!' Fanny cried with amazement as she opened the door. 'What on earth are you doing here?'

'I don't care what Father says. I'm fed up. We spend all day alone in the house and I want to come to school. Please will you teach us in secret? I'm not afraid to come here. Mother did and I don't believe in soppy old ghosts!'

'Vanessa, are you sure you know what you're asking? We'd be disobeying your father.'

'But I want to learn, Miss Crowe. Please teach us.'

Fanny sighed and stared down at the perplexed child. 'Well, if you're sure you know what you want, I know a place where we won't be disturbed,' the teacher replied, still slightly warily. But in spite of all that Blackburn had said, or perhaps even because of it, she agreed to teach the girls in secret, three afternoons a week after school.

The following afternoon, as they set off towards the cool, shady fern gully, there was a certain nervousness amongst them.

'I do hope nobody sees us,' Vanessa said as she and Fanny walked on, slightly ahead of Clarissa. 'Father was really very angry last night. But it seems so unfair. We have no one to talk to.'

Clarissa, more reticent, dragged along behind. She felt very uncomfortable with the deception. Hadn't their father already shouted at them the previous evening? She could not fathom why Vanessa should want to pursue this desire. She watched her sister gaily chattering to Fanny as they led the way along the mountain path.

The gully was indeed as pretty and as hidden as Fanny had promised them. The girls settled down with their new teacher under the shade of some long arching fern fronds. Fanny was feeling in very good spirits. This was to be her first French lesson since leaving England. She began to unpack her textbooks with enthusiasm, noticing that although Vanessa was keen to learn, Clarissa was reluctant. She watched the younger girl lean back against the tall trunk of the tree fern and rest her cheek against the soft bark. The girl was reserved, even withdrawn. 'Probably fearful of her father,' Fanny deduced. She tried not to allow this to trouble her. 'I so hope I can win her trust,' Fanny thought to herself. She felt a slight worry that the child's feelings would betray their complicity.

'Now, I need to know what you have learned so far.'

'I know the word for pen is *le plume*,' Vanessa answered with enthusiasm. Clarissa turned towards her sister. She saw how eagerly she participated.

'*La*, not *le*. It is feminine. Do you both know that all nouns in French have a gender?'

'I can sing in French, Miss Crowe,' Clarissa piped

up. And she proudly begun to hum 'La Marseillaise'.

'Humming is not French, young lady! I think we'd better start with lesson one.'

Fanny, much amused, picked up her beginner's grammar book. The three sat huddled together, intently leaning close over the one book, surrounded by the mountain perfumes. The fresh creek water gurgled happily at their side.

From behind a huge boulder, positioned slightly above them, Richard could see his two sisters with their teacher. Although he could hear nothing of what was being said, he saw them laughing. It appeared that Fanny was working with them and reading to them. They seemed to be thoroughly enjoying themselves, he thought. He stayed watching them for a while, wondering what she might be teaching them, fascinated by what they could be laughing about.

Suddenly he realised he had lost track of the time. 'It must have been several hours since Father sent me to the village store,' he thought. 'Now I'll be in trouble, reprimanded again for dawdling.' He stood up and brushed the dust and bracken from his trousers. 'I'll tell Father what I've just seen, that'll appease him. Or maybe I should wait, to keep him in a good mood for the last part of the afternoon, and tell him in the wagon on the way home from the paddocks.'

Richard climbed down from his hiding place and started making his way back down the path. Earlier in the afternoon he had had a confrontation with Patrick. It had left him feeling awkward and unhappy. He kicked his feet in the dust crossly as he slouched along the path. He was really fed up about it. Patrick had always been his closest companion. They had spent a great deal of their time together. Patrick, being two years his senior and the more daring of the couple, had been a splendid teacher as well as a fine excuse for being allowed more adventurous activities.

As he walked back now, dragging his heels, knowing he should be hurrying, he thought back to the time they had gone shooting together and Patrick had saved his life . . .

'Jeez, I was nearly strangled by that snake! I thought I'd shot it.' He remembered hurling the dead thing around his neck to carry home in triumph when suddenly it started moving, slowly winding itself tighter around his throat. He was choking and couldn't call out. Patrick had noticed what was happening and had run to his rescue. Finally, as Richard had gasped for breath, the odious creature was uncurled and shot dead. Patrick had indeed saved him. . .

Why were they enemies now? They had drifted apart these last few weeks. Since the damned old hotel had been rebuilt. This afternoon at the general store was the worst. Richard was regretting his actions now. He had not wanted to fight with Pat. If his father had not sent him on those stupid errands none of this would have happened. He had no idea why he'd ganged up with those boys. He didn't even like them. He had just arrived in the village after his lunch and he'd seen them shouting names at Patrick, calling him a traitor for going to school. He had watched them for a moment and then joined in adding to Pat's provocation. 'Why did I have to shout too?' he thought now. 'I didn't mean to hurt him.' The Irish boy had been holding his tongue until he saw Richard join in with the gang. And then Pat had lashed out, abruptly grabbing Richard and hurling him onto the dusty street. They had begun to scrap and shout abuse at one another. Most of the other boys had held back. It had become a fight between the two friends.

Patrick had called him a cissy. That had hurt him.

He had shouted back at Patrick, 'You're only going to school 'cos your brother makes you! She's evil, that woman, living there!'

'Yeah! She's a witch!' the other boys had shouted, taunting Patrick.

'You're just a coward! You're weak!' Pat turned on Richard. 'You do anything your father tells you. You never think for yourself.'

That had hurt him, too. He had been too hurt to say anything. 'Perhaps I am a coward,' he thought now.

Then, he remembered, his friend had thrown him against the timber verandah of the store, and he had fallen on his face. It had stung and made his nose bleed, but Pat had just walked away. The others had jeered at Richard's defeat. He had picked himself up and walked into the store to collect the provisions feeling sore from the beating and mortified by the humiliation . . .

Now, he hurried along the path towards the paddock where his restless father would be waiting. Dusk was falling as he fled nervously along the lane, puffing and panting the last few tired yards.

'Blast!' He'll be furious,' the boy moaned, silently berating himself for his wasted afternoon. To his horror he saw the first group of labourers walking towards him commencing their weary journeys homeward.

'Your pa's waitin' on you, young Richard,' one young scruffy lad shouted to him as they passed in the lane.

Richard began to run even faster until suddenly he spotted the dreaded wagon approaching. Automatically he slowed down, choosing to wait where he was, to give himself a moment to collect his thoughts and think of an excuse. The wagon drew closer. Henry, seeing his son idling in the lane, drew on the reins.

'Where the hell've you been? Did you think I'd wait all night!' his father shouted angrily. 'Get in!' The admonished boy clambered into the wagon, passing the provisions over into the back. 'What kept you so long?'

'Had to wait while ol' Burnley unpacked new stock,' the boy lied uncomfortably.

'Mmm,' Blackburn retorted.

They rode on together in silence lost in their warm dusk tiredness. Richard was glad that the moment had passed painlessly. Henry was burdened with weightier sorrows . . .

'You're very quiet, eh. Something on your mind?' Henry asked after a time, oblivious now to his earlier anger.

Hearing a softer note in Blackburn's voice, the boy knew now was the time to tell his father about his sisters and Fanny sitting together at the creek. Laughing.

'I saw something, that's all.'

'What?'

Richard paused, about to tell his father what he had seen. But as he deliberated, the sound of Pat's voice calling him a coward reverberated through his mind. He saw in his mind his sisters, with Fanny, sitting on the grass enjoying themselves.

'Well, what did you see?' his father pressed, a little impatiently.

'Old Jeremiah. Snooping about.' It was not entirely a lie. He had seen the shrivelled old man wandering about near the haunted school. It was true that he had looked as if he was snooping.

'Around our land, was he? I told him before to damn well keep away! You tell him, if he comes by again, I'll shoot him in cold blood!'

'Yes, Father,' said Richard, maintaining his secret, glad now that he might not be such a coward.

Several afternoons later Fanny retreated once more to her favourite spot under the tree ferns. Engrossed as she was, alone with her new book, she did not hear the approaching horse hooves.

Joseph pulled on the reins and the mare obediently halted. Through the drooping leaves, swaying lightly in the afternoon breeze, he spied the schoolteacher. He watched her for a moment, observing her in repose, unself-consciously turning the pages of her book. Fanny's curly chestnut hair blew untidily about her face. Joseph dismounted. As he let go of the reins the bay drifted a short distance to feed herself. He walked towards Fanny who, disturbed by the footsteps, looked up. He sat down beside her on the grass. For a moment they were silent.

'I haven't seen you for a few days,' Joseph said

eventually. 'Pat says you have four pupils this week.'

'Yes, I have. Two brothers arrived from across the valley. Their name is Watkinson.'

'Yes, I know them. They're a good family. You must be feeling more content with life now.' He watched her, her head still lowered to her book, idly picking at a blade of grass. 'What's that you're reading, Fanny?'

'This? It's *Great Expectations*. An English novel, published just before I left home. It's written by a man called Charles Dickens. I enjoy his books,' she laughed, lightly stroking the cover of her book. 'Whenever I was not kept too busy by my father I would sneak off to the shop,' she giggled naughtily, 'and buy his most recent story. Then I'd hurry home and take it up to my room and stay reading there until suppertime.' Fanny placed the book on the grass. 'He's a very modern writer, very English. It seems a long time ago now,' she added wistfully.

Joseph looked towards the novel, knowing all the pages held secrets closed to him. He would have liked to talk to Fanny about the book. He saw how reading delighted her.

'Do you miss England, Fanny?'

'No, not really. Although sometimes I think of it, remember things. Not many people, though. I only had one relative still alive when I left. A ferocious old aunt called Alice.' She looked up and smiled at him, sharing her silly conspiracy. 'I haven't written to her, except to say that I'd arrived safely. She disapproved of my coming here.' She paused for a moment. He watched her daydreaming of that distant land. 'Yesterday I was thinking that it's almost a year since I left. It was just before Christmas. It'll be strange to spend it here, all alone, no snow!' she teased. 'I suppose I'll write a letter to my aunt for Christmas. Tell her about my school.' She stopped her chatter, fell silent again and dipped her fingers into the cool mountain water.

'What about you, Joseph?' She glanced up at him. 'Do you miss Ireland then?'

'Me?' he laughed. 'It's so long since I was there I hardly remember the place. I left with my parents when I was a boy just after the famines. 'Twas a terrible time. My mother died on the boat giving birth to Pat. Then later, in Sydney, my father died. I was still less than twenty. He was a kid. I've brought him up on my own ever since. Here. This has been where we've survived. We'd have starved to death in Ireland.' He looked about him at the mountains surrounding them. 'This is my land now, Fanny. This untamed place has given me a life. Shown me there's another way, a chance for us all. I'm Australian now, Fanny.' He lifted his hand to stroke her hair, and teased her saying, 'Just as you will be, Miss Crowe, when you settle yourself.'

'What do you mean by settle myself? And it's

very improper to touch a lady. Please remember your place and don't do that again.' She was feeling flustered and confused but did not wish him to see it. She rose quickly, saying, 'It's high time I walked back to my school. I have plenty to do there. Goodbye, Joseph.'

With that she was gone, hurrying anxiously down to the village. Joseph stood up, intending to escort her, or offer his mare. Then he saw her precious book lying in the grass, completely forgotten. He picked it up and considered whether to call her back but instead he slipped it into his belt and walked to his chestnut mare.

Richard, although unable to hear any of what had passed between Fanny and Joseph, had observed the encounter. He had been stalking Fanny all the afternoon and had still been furtively watching her when Joseph arrived. He saw Fanny hurry off but thought it best not to follow. It seemed safer to wait behind the gum trees until Joseph was well out of sight. He certainly did not want to be caught – particularly by Patrick's brother.

As he waited there amongst the trees, wondering why Fanny had disappeared so abruptly as they did not seem to have been quarrelling, he was startled by a sound behind him. It sounded like approaching footsteps cracking on the bracken. He crouched low, still as a rabbit, hoping that whoever was walking in the woods would not pass by him, whoever it might be. He did not want to be discovered. He already felt a giddy guilt, having spent the whole afternoon following her. He could not explain why he had. He did not know why. His sisters had not been in her company. He just wanted to watch her. Perhaps he would discover why others thought she was evil.

The footsteps were coming closer. He was about to be seen! He looked about him. There was no other spot, nothing more concealed. Perhaps someone would tell his father. The figure was behind him. He could hear the breathing, wheezing more like.

'Well, well! It's young Richard Blackburn. Spying? Is that your game?'

The boy froze. He was not able to turn around. He knew the voice only too well, although he himself had rarely engaged in conversation with the owner of the unpleasant growl.

'What brings you here? If it's not snooping?'

Without turning his head to confront the ugly old man, Richard stood up and answered with hardly more than a whisper. 'I was searching for stray lambs and . . .' he coughed mid-sentence,'and I lost my own way a little.' He sensed his lie as utterly unconvincing.

'Lambs 'ere?' retorted the growl. 'You know as well as me they never wander up 'ere. You were spying on the witch!' Such a statement amazed Richard so entirely that he turned to face his forest companion.

'Did you call Miss Crowe a witch? I don't think that's true!'

'Your mother was killed by my brother's ghost,' said Jeremiah. 'Yet she lives on there unharmed. 'ow do you account for that?'

Richard stared at the gnarled old goldminer, and considered carefully the implication of what the old man had said. Indeed his father had said several times that Fanny must be entirely wicked to live in such a place. It was also widely believed in the village. He had even said it himself to Patrick when they were fighting. Somehow, though, she just did not look like a witch.

'I know my mother died there. I can't see how that makes Miss Crowe a witch.'

'You just don't want to believe it! I've told you often my brother lives there. 'e frequently tells me he'll be revenged on any who go there. I still see the wounds that mutilated 'is body. 'e was murdered there. You all know it. No one but your mother was foolish enough to disregard 'is warnings and she paid for it with 'er life. How do you think this woman lives there? 'ow can she survive where no one else can?'

'But it doesn't make her a witch!' Richard was uncertain why he was fighting so hard for Fanny's reputation.

104

'She's in commune with the devil to keep 'er safe. One day I'll show you. Your mother was a good woman, eh? Yet the evil spirit got 'er. He'll get anyone who goes there. 'e was a Christian man who died without a chance to make his peace. He walks unsettled. What kind of woman can live with that and be at peace with 'erself? Think of your mother, Richard, and think what this school teacher must be. She's evil. She should be driven away from 'ere.'

Jeremiah had been drawing closer to Richard as he spoke. Richard had never heard him speak so much before, or so passionately. The ugliness of his words and face and his sheer proximity created a fear in the boy. Although he was terrified he was transfixed. The old hermit drew even closer. He smelt horrible and his grinning teeth were black.

Suddenly the boy fled from his presence. He ran as fast as he could down through the wooded paths. He no longer concerned himself with being seen. Anything was better than the company of that horrible old man.

❖ CHAPTER SEVEN ❖

Alone in his room that night, Richard prepared for bed and rain began to fall outside in the valley. He hurriedly pulled off his shirt and pants, carelessly throwing them onto a chair, and paused, listening to the storm forcefully beat against the trees. In the dim shadowy light he moved listlessly over to the window, knelt naked on the cushioned window seat and peered out. It was difficult to see anything. The entire valley seemed to be engulfed in mist. When he pressed his face close against the glass he could just about make out the swaying trees as the rain now lashed against them forcing them earthwards.

His attention was drawn to a long dark insect, rather like a dragonfly, balanced against the window frame. Its body moved slowly up and down as though pulled by a string. He watched it, mesmerised by its rhythmical movement until, as the rain beat faster and more furiously, the creature was knocked off balance and disappeared from sight. Richard remained, fretfully gazing out into the screened, sodden darkness. The image of Jeremiah's ugly threatening face would not dismiss itself from his mind. Restlessly he crossed the room and got into bed.

He lay listening to the cascade of rain pounding on the roof. The wind howling through the valley, with the high-pitched scream of some distressed creature, sounded to him like the wail of Jeremiah's murdered brother. He heard his father leave the study and wearily climb the stairs. The landing creaked, Henry's bedroom door closed, and the house fell silent, save for the furious night outside. Staring at the ceiling, Richard pictured Amos Johnson with his scarred, mutilated body, perhaps at that very moment, stalking the old hotel. He rolled over and buried his frightened face in the pillow, desperate for rest. He felt as though he were the only creature in the world still awake. He closed his eyes, forcing himself to sleep, but instead he saw the old mahogany brown miner with his mad staring eyes talking of Amos haunting the hotel. Richard, as fearful as if the ghost were there with him in the room, lay trembling, knowing there was no one he could turn to. If he told his story he would have to admit that he had been discovered spying on the schoolteacher. Caught by Jeremiah.

His mind drifted to Fanny. Was she really a witch? His father had said she was wicked. It was true that his mother had died at the old hotel, while the schoolteacher remained safe. Was she able to safeguard herself against the spirits because she too was evil? Because she was a witch? How would he know? He had never seen a witch. He *had* to find out the truth. He longed for his mother to be with him, saying goodnight to him, helping him go to sleep by stroking his forehead, soothing his fears. She would have understood.

Richard curled up into a ball and slid down deep into the bed, hoping and praying that if he closed his eyes tightly enough all of his fears would go away. He did not want to think about these things any longer. Just to sleep. And slowly his desire became real. He drifted off with eyes shut tight. Eventually all thoughts of ghosts and witches were dispelled for the night and the lonely, confused boy slept peacefully.

A clap of thunder distracted Fanny's attention. She closed her book tight and sighed deeply. Propped up against her pillow, she listened to the storm outside. A leak dribbling through the small square window caught her attention. It ran down the inside of the pane, along the narrow sill and dripped onto the floor.

'That will drive me mad!' she muttered crossly

and leapt from her bed, searching impatiently around her little room. She found an old white petticoat and flung it onto the floor under the window, then climbed back into bed and watched the water run down onto the mass of white calico. She was feeling ill-tempered with herself for her foolishness, for fleeing from Joseph and for leaving her precious Charles Dickens book in the grass. By the time she had realised it was still at the gully it had been too dark to return for it. Anyway the sky had looked grey and ominous and she was already comfortably settled in her schoolroom making notes for the next day's lessons. 'I will fetch it tomorrow,' she had promised herself.

Now, as she lay in her little bed, another book in her slender white hand, still chiding herself for her foolish behaviour and listening to the rain spilling down the hill behind the school and running in small rivulets alongside the building, she began to doze. In her sleepy state she heard occasional voices calling to one another across the village. Folk running in the rain as they hurried to their homes after drinking late at Joshua Burnley's store.

Suddenly in her half-waking, half-sleeping state she was roused by the abrupt sound of something thudding. She awoke with a terrified jolt and then saw that it was only her book, which had fallen to the floor. She leaned over the side of the bed to pick it up again. As she put it on her bedside table she mocked herself for her foolish fear. 'For one moment,' she teased, 'I thought I'd heard a ghost! I almost believed that mad old man!' She turned down the kerosene lamp, chuckling, and settled herself comfortably under the covers, ready for sleep.

Silence descended upon Moogalloo and the surrounding hills and valleys. The rain settled into a steady drum, disturbing no one, almost comforting in its constancy. The whole world lay sleeping. It seemed that nothing moved, that even the creatures of the night lay still, fearful of another outburst from the sky.

Within the sleeping stillness of this drenched village a sound – not the steady beating of rain, not the occasional crack of branches falling to the sodden earth, but another indefinable sound, emanated from the old hotel. Something was moving in the ruins of the old, cursed building.

Fanny woke with a start. She had heard something again and it wasn't her book. She sat up in bed, listening, hardly daring to breathe, too frightened to light the lamp. She waited. The rain seemed to have eased. An owl hooted somewhere in the distance. Perhaps she had been dreaming. Her encounter with Joseph had unsettled her. Perhaps that had disturbed her sleep. But this was the second time tonight she had felt frightened.

Perhaps there *was* something or someone there, moving about in the old building. What had woken her? Why did she feel so frightened? All the nights she had been sleeping there she had never entertained ideas of evil spirits. She had always scoffed such notions. Yet tonight it felt different . . . Try as she might, she could not convince herself there was nothing there. She was certain something had been moving. She wanted to get out of bed, creep into the schoolroom, but she dare not. She could not move her limbs.

'Can it really be?' she asked herself impatiently, 'that after all this time you are going to believe this nonsense? Fanny, if you are truly afraid, then get out of bed this instant and see for yourself that only your dreams have woken you!' She took a deep breath, and turned down the crocheted cover. As she lifted her unwilling leg a scratching, shuffling noise came from the next room.

'There *is* something there!' she shuddered, grasping the front of her nightdress. 'Oh, I wish I were in England!'

She sat on the side of the bed and held resolutely onto her wooden table. It was for strength rather than to light the lamp. She could not decide whether she should fumble her way in the dark or carry the lamp. It seemed an insurmountable decision. Finally she decided to search without the lamp. As she rose and walked stealthily to the

111

schoolroom door, the scuffling, burrowing sound ceased.

'Nevertheless, Fanny, you are going to see this through!' She opened the schoolroom door and closed her eyes, terrified of what she might see. She took another deep breath and said a silent prayer. She cautiously opened one eye, then the second and slowly, carefully scanned the room. There was nothing there. Only desk and benches sitting empty, waiting for the next day's school, damp patches on the floor where drips had leaked through the ceiling, and drops of rain clinging eerily to the windows.

Fanny breathed a long, deep sigh and scurried back to bed, deciding to sleep, for safety, with the door open.

'At least I can see if something's coming,' she told herself unconvincingly. 'It must have been a wombat, or some such night creature, searching for shelter from the downpour. Heaven only knows what creatures live under the building or in the roof. Certainly not ghosts!'

She lay down on the bed without covering herself, feeling foolish for her silly notions, yet praying for morning just the same. There was no doubt about it. Something in the creaking building had unnerved her.

❖ CHAPTER EIGHT ❖

It was a warm, sunny Sunday morning in Moogalloo. The surrounding hills were dressed with vegetation, lush and colourful from the recent rains. Within the village and the hillside homesteads, people were busily preparing themselves for chapel. Best Sunday clothes were being donned after hair had been combed and nails and faces had been scrubbed. There was the usual Sunday air of urgency. Families were setting off in good time, across the valley and through the bush, on foot, horseback or in loaded wagons. This once-a-week ritual was for many of the locals a social gathering, an opportunity to gossip or chatter at leisure, content in the knowledge that another week's toil had been completed and another Sunday lunch had been earned.

In the village itself Joshua Burnley, the old bald-headed storekeeper, had thrown away all thoughts of accounts for the week, left his apron on the counter and was happily scrubbing his shop-soiled hands. He hummed to himself as he vigorously dried his wet arms, put the towel on his wooden dining table, strolled over to the window, lifted the worn lace curtain and peered out. This solitary old widower was a creature of habit. He could set his watch by the rituals he paced out. Every Sunday morning he spied Reverend Dalton hurrying across the square, making his way back to the chapel after a brisk morning walk. The bow-legged, preoccupied pastor, hand on flying hat, was always to be seen scurrying across the dusty street at this time.

Burnley turned away from the window, chuckling to himself and picked up his jacket from the chair. 'Must be ten past ten. Time for chapel,' he thought proudly. He lovingly lifted his treasured silver fob-watch from his jacket pocket, held it in his creased old hand and gazed at its neat white face. It was indeed precisely ten minutes after ten.

'S'pose pastor's worryin' about the time agin!' chuckled Burnley, gleefully wiping his spectacles with the discarded towel.

'Dear Lord!' thought Reverend Dalton. 'I do hope I'm not late!' He puffed his way up to the chapel, pushed open the creaking wooden door and hurried up the narrow, silent aisle, to quietly await his small, faithful congregation. In spite of his concern, he was always the first to arrive, save for whichever local wife had visited earlier to dust the hard wooden pews and arrange a display of

114

motley bush flowers. Dalton bent reverently and placed his black hat on the stone floor beside the altar. He lifted his bulky chapel Bible and proceeded to turn the yellowing pages in search of his chosen morning lesson.

Things were different out at *Rosewood*. Since the death of Maria, Henry had not encouraged churchgoing within his family. He himself had never been one for 'attending services or being preached at' but had, in the past, tolerated it for the sake of his wife. As a Catholic, Maria had insisted that her family receive some formal religious education. Occasionally she had even persuaded Henry to accompany her and the children. He acquiesced, believing it kept her happy. It certainly pleased the three youngsters. They would stand with an extra glow of pride if their father was at their side. He was, after all, much respected and much feared in the community.

But since Maria's death, it was one more custom or habit that had disappeared from *Rosewood*. Henry now insisted that his daughters prepare his breakfast on Sundays, just as they did every other day of the week. Although he set off for work later on Sunday mornings, preferring to enjoy a leisurely meal of eggs, soda bread and sometimes devilled kidneys, he did still continue to oversee land duties. 'The land has to be maintained and the sheep have to be fed, no matter what day of the week. I've no regard for the sabbath. The beasts feeding on my land are hungry seven days a week,' was a motto he lived by and constantly quoted.

Richard and Clarissa finished laying mugs on the table and sat in their chairs to await the arrival of breakfast. Vanessa carried the laden tray from the scullery into the family kitchen and placed the plates on the cedarwood table. She sat down as the family silently commenced eating.

'And what have you two done this past week?' Henry Blackburn asked his daughters. 'I've seen little of you out in the paddocks.'

Richard passed his father a portion of the soda loaf, baked the previous day by Liza Roundway. As he did so he watched his sisters carefully, knowing they had spent a deal of their time with the schoolteacher, Fanny Crowe. He awaited their reply with interest.

The two sisters glanced at one another, exchanging a conspiratorial secret. Clarissa shifted uncomfortably in her chair.

'Mrs Roundway has been showing us new things in the kitchen. She has promised to teach me bread baking and pickling,' Vanessa answered. It was a tiny white lie, unnoticed by Henry. She was already a fine young cook. She feared, as she crossed her fingers under the table, that Clarissa may become nervous and tell something of the

116

truth. Richard caught Clarissa's eyes, intrigued to know what she was going to say. The small blonde girl looked guiltily down at her plate.

'And what of you, Clarissa? What have you done with your time?'

Vanessa eyed her younger sister fervently. There was a mere second's encouragement in the gaze, which Richard could perceive but which went unnoticed by their father.

'We walked together a few times,' the younger girl piped up, encouraged by her sister's confident example.

'Oh aye, and whereabouts were you walking?' Henry asked idly, more involved in his breakfast.

'Up by the creek, mostly,' replied Clarissa, rather too honestly for Vanessa's comfort.

'What's so interestin' there? It's quite a way from here.' Henry busily chewed his sheep's kidneys.

'It's cool to sit there in the heat of the sun,' replied the elder daughter instantly.

'No sense walking all the way up there in the hot sun to find somewhere cool to sit! Better to stay here. Or come with Richard and me. Some days we're near the river. You can sit there.' He continued munching his way heartily through his breakfast, oblivious to the scene in front of him. 'Not that I've seen much of you this week, Richard. Searchin' for the stray lambs seems to have kept you mightily busy,' Henry accused sarcastically as he dug into the breakfast plate once more.

Richard said nothing. No answer seemed to be required.

'I hope you've not seen that schoolmistress again? Richard, have you seen these two with her since I forbade it?' The girls both cowered and glanced nervously at their brother. Neither could be certain if he had guessed their deceit.

'No, Papa, not since they came to the valley with her.' He hated lying to his father. But what alternative had he now? He himself had spent too many hours following Fanny. Several of those hours she had passed with his sisters. He longed to know what they were learning. He only knew they were deceiving their father. But he had his own deceit too. How could he say anything? He no longer wanted to betray them. He no longer wanted to betray her. He was fascinated by her, and longed to know the truth about her.

As soon as breakfast was over and Henry had set off in his wagon, Richard skipped hastily from the house. His lie had left him feeling uneasy in the presence of his family. As soon as he was out of sight he slowed down, walking lazily towards the village. In the old days he would have gone to chapel. Later he and Patrick might have gone off to fish or hunt but those days seemed long since past. Life felt very different now.

As he approached the village he saw Joseph and

Pat walking towards the chapel, chatting, both looking smart and clean. He had not seen his friend of late, not since the fight between them outside Burnley's store. He did not, in his present frame of mind, want to face him. Quickly he turned down one of the narrow dusty slipways that led away from the village centre and waited there, in hiding, for a minute or two. He decided he would creep to the side wall of the chapel and listen to the hymns. He had always enjoyed singing the hymns. Sometimes at *Rosewood*, in the evening after supper, his mother had played the piano whilst he and his sisters had sung for their father.

After enough time had elapsed for the two Irish brothers to have settled in the chapel, he left his hiding place and retraced his steps along the path. A rustle in the brush on the hillside above caught his attention. He looked up and spied Jeremiah creeping suspiciously along the path. Richard hung back cautiously watching the old man. He seemed to be carrying something, some sort of pole, but from that distance it was hard for Richard to see clearly what it might be.

'He's on his way to the old hotel!' That much seemed clear to the boy. The old scruffy prospector paused momentarily behind some bracken, glanced about him cautiously and then stole in a little closer. He peered down towards the back of the building. Richard assumed he must be looking to see if it was occupied by the schoolteacher. 'What's he carrying?' the boy asked himself. He longed to move closer but dare not, lest he be spied himself.

At that moment the schoolroom door was opened. Fanny stepped out onto the verandah. She was becomingly dressed in her Sunday clothes, ready for chapel. Richard's attention was instantly drawn to her. He quite forgot the old man, who had heard the footsteps and had withdrawn anyway.

'How pretty she looks, not like an old witch at all!' Fanny was dressed in a green frock with cream lace. Richard longed to accompany her to chapel. He watched her close her schoolroom door and pause for a moment on the verandah. She lifted a bonnet to her head and tied it in place over her chestnut curls. This done, she slipped on her cream gloves, stepped down from the verandah, and walked hurriedly across the street, making her late way to the service.

That simple moment had reminded Richard of many Sundays. Sundays when he and his sisters had accompanied their mother, sometimes their father too, and together they had ridden in the wagon to chapel. This private longing for his past carefree life had so overwhelmed him that he clean forgot the antics of Jeremiah.

He turned and walked away from the village in

any direction except home. He wandered aimlessly for a while feeling sullen and sorry for himself. Sometimes running, sometimes walking, he gradually made his way up the mountainside until, exhausted and out of breath, he threw himself down by the creek, under the very ferns where he had so recently watched Fanny with his sisters. Tired and sad, he lay down on the grass and within a short time fell fast asleep.

Inside the chapel the last hymn of the morning sounded in the congregation's ears. All who had attended the service shuffled towards the gnarled old wooden door and bade their farewells and thank yous to Reverend Dalton for his splendid service. Joshua Burnley shook Dalton's hand and said, as he did every week, 'Very uplifting, Reverend.' He nodded politely to Fanny, who stood engaged in conversation with Dalton, then he set off towards his store. The community drifted its leisurely, Sunday way across the village to their various homes or huddled together in groups to chatter in the warm, late morning sunlight. Fanny bid the pastor good morning and stepped out into the brilliant sunshine, removing her bonnet as she did so, and nodding occasionally to a familiar or inquisitive face.

'Fanny, I thought I'd take the liberty of calling on you this morning,' Joseph called out to her as he walked towards her and then alongside her.

Fanny was surprised by his formality. She had temporarily forgotten the scene that had occurred between them so few days ago.

'Joseph,' she laughed, 'Of course you may. I'd be pleased to see you. In fact I'm going for a picnic later and thought you might like to join me. We could, all three, set off together.'

'Alas, I have to ride to Benningee. I want to return your book, though.'

Fanny stopped and turned to him. She was beaming with pleasure. 'Oh, Joseph, did you find it? I was utterly desolate thinking that I'd lost it in the grass. And when I returned the next day it had gone. I thought I would never know the end of the story.' She clapped her gloved hands together, freely expressing her delight. 'Please Joseph, bring it to me before you set off for Benningee and then I can take it with me on my picnic.'

Smiling she turned to Patrick, who stood waiting at a distance for his brother. 'What about you, Patrick? Would you like to come walking with me and help me eat my picnic lunch?'

'I promised to meet Richard,' he lied hastily. He felt no desire to go walking with Fanny. Five mornings of school were quite enough for him. He liked her well enough but he felt much less comfortable with her these days, since she had insisted that he call her Miss Crowe. It was confusing.

Now he never knew when to call her Fanny and when to call her Miss Crowe.

As they reached the school verandah Fanny stepped out of the sun, onto the porch. 'You promise to call before you leave for Benningee, then?'

'Certainly. I have an idea! It's an offer of another pupil,' Joseph said mischievously, with a gleam in his blue eyes as he and his brother turned towards their own wooden home.

A short while later Joseph banged enthusiastically on Fanny's schoolroom door.

'Here's your precious book, safe and sound,' he said, and turned from the delighted schoolteacher and mounted his waiting chestnut mare.

'Oh, Joseph, wait! Please don't go without telling me who's to be my new pupil,' she cried, excited with anticipation.

'Why, Fanny, didn't you guess? It's me, of course!' Joseph laughed heartily, his warm face beaming with pleasure as he tipped his hat, swung the bay around, and rode off at full gallop towards Benningee.

'What a surprise!' thought Fanny, as she hurried along, up to her favourite spot by the creek, carrying her treasured Charles Dickens close to her dress. 'Fancy Joseph wanting to read and write!' She had hastily prepared her simple picnic and was now carrying it along in her basket. She longed for her shady gully and for several hours alone, with only Pip and Magwitch to keep her company. 'What a motley bunch I'm gathering for my school!' She was delighted to have an extra pupil and secretly even more so because it was Joseph. She had never realised he would care to learn.

Fanny arrived at her treasured, tranquil spot, hidden from the judging eyes of the village, and bent to avoid the low drooping fronds of the tree ferns as she stepped into the gully. She paused in amazement as she saw Richard Blackburn lying asleep on the grass, his jacket under his head for a pillow. 'I wonder what he's doing here?' she asked herself as she crept up beside him.

She gazed intently down at his sleeping face, then placed her basket on the grass, stealthily unfolded a blanket and sat down at his side. She rummaged for her book, careful not to wake him, found her page and proceeded to read.

After some twenty pages or so she began to feel very hungry but decided to wait for Richard to wake before unpacking her picnic. Suddenly he began to stir. She heard him moan lightly under his breath and watched him as he gradually opened his sleepy eyes and looked about him, trying to recollect where he was. She found it endearing to watch him. After the few moments it took him to recall his whereabouts he lifted himself up onto his elbows and was startled to see her sitting at his side. Fanny closed her book, leaving one slender finger in the page to keep her place, and smiled warmly at him.

'It's quite a surprise, a lovely one, to find you here. This is my favourite spot in the mountains. I have been sitting here reading for a while and am now very hungry. You must be, too. I thought you might like to share my picnic?'

Richard said nothing. He felt a little puzzled.

'It seemed a trifle rude to just eat everything while you were sleeping, so I decided to wait for you.' Without waiting for an answer, Fanny proceeded to unwrap the cloth from the top of the basket. That was to be their picnic table. Richard watched her lay it on the grass. 'Perhaps you could take the other side, Richard. Help to make it flat.'

He obeyed as quietly as one of his father's newborn lambs.

'We have a small portion of chicken each, but there is only one container for water, I'm afraid. I wasn't expecting guests! But we do have plenty of bananas. It's quite simple, but there's plenty for two.' She unwrapped the cold boiled chicken and passed a leg to the hungry, silent, bemused boy. He took it warily but, once in his hand, he ate heartily. 'I'm delighted to have this chance to spend a little time with you,' she said.

Fanny hardly touched her food, being more involved in watching him. She was curious about the Blackburns. She rose with the container in her hand and bent down to the creek to fill the mug with the clear water.

She turned to him and said with a smile, 'I was hoping you might have come to school by now. I was certain you would have persuaded your father to let you attend. I wish you would. Nothing would please me more.' She returned to her spot on the grass and handed him the container.

'Thank you,' he said gingerly and bit into the chicken once more, a little more timidly this time. 'I told you, Father says we can't come to school. He thinks you're wicked.'

Fanny felt that his commitment to this belief was not as strong as when she had visited him at *Rosewood*.

'Can't you see how silly it is to call me wicked? Surely you see that for yourself?' she laughed, teasingly. 'What reason could there possibly be for believing that?' She giggled at the idea of her own wickedness and began, happily, to peel the skin from her chicken leg. She had not expected him to answer, so was quite unprepared for the accusation that followed.

'What are you laughing at? My mother was killed at your horrible school and you live there

126

with the ghost that killed her. Everybody says you'd have been driven away by now if you weren't evil and if there wasn't some evil spirit looking after you!'

'Richard!' cried Fanny. 'That is absurd! There is no ghost. That's why I'm safe in the hotel. It's just superstition. There is nothing there to hurt me.'

'Then how d'you s'pose my mother died? I saw her!' he cried. He did not wait for an answer, just leapt to his feet and threw the half-eaten bone onto the tablecloth. 'I hate you!' he shouted at Fanny. Then he ran from the gully as fast as he could.

Fanny stood up, immediately calling after him as loud as she could, but it was too late. His passion had sped him away from her. She was desolate. She had not intended her frivolity and teasing to cause him pain. She sat down again and began dispiritedly to pack away her picnic. It had seemed such a good idea to her less than an hour ago.

She spent most of the rest of the afternoon sitting restlessly amongst the bracken, occasionally returning to her book, but in her present frame of mind it held no joy for her. As she considered preparing to leave she heard the soft canter of hooves on the nearby dust path. Her instinct told her that it might be Joseph. She was not aware how desperately she wanted it to be him. As the horse approached the nearby clump of wattle bushes she saw it was indeed Joseph's chestnut mare. She leapt to her feet and ran eagerly to meet him.

'Oh Joseph, I'm so glad to see you. I've had such a horrible afternoon!'

He dismounted instantly, letting the reins drop, and left the animal to graze at leisure.

'What is it?' he said, taking her by the arms. 'What's happened?'

Fanny, without thinking of the consequences of her action, flung herself against her friend and began to weep. She poured out the whole story: how she had teased Richard and how he had thought she was laughing at him; how she had failed in her attempt to create a bond with the boy; how she hated the idea that others judged and despised her; and, more particularly, how she was afraid that now Richard would hate her.

Joseph silently listened to her outburst. When he sensed her tears were over he held onto her tightly, saying tenderly, 'Shhh, Fanny, Fanny, Fanny. We'll overcome their prejudice, I promise you. It takes time, that's all. Now, please stop the crying. I've got some good news. Today, you have not only me as a new pupil. Whilst I was in Benningee I persuaded a local couple to send their children to school too. They can't be there all the time but they've agreed that whenever they go off to market to sell their produce, they'll leave the two boys with you. Now, Fanny,' he continued before she could interrupt. 'I know teaching pupils once in a while is not your idea of a proper school, but it's better than no pupils, so dry your eyes.'

Fanny, in a most unladylike fashion, dabbed her face with the lace on her sleeve. She felt a little ashamed at her outburst and wished that Joseph would let go of her arms. As delicately as she was able she disengaged herself and returned to her spot on the grass.

'I behaved rather foolishly, Joseph. Please excuse me.' She placed her book in the basket.

'Fanny, please try to see that I want to help you. If you would only really let me,' he said, crouching beside her. 'Fanny, if you would allow me, we could work together, build your little school together. Don't you . . . realise . . . how I feel . . .'

Without allowing him to say any more, Fanny turned on him. 'Joseph, I have told you before, I appreciate your kindness but your intimacy is quite out of place. We are two very different people. It is most improper for a lady of my station to talk this way with you.' She picked up her basket and stood up, turning to face him directly. 'I shall ask you, please, never to speak to me in such a way again.'

For just a moment he said nothing. She saw the anger burning brilliantly in his usually kind blue eyes.

'Whatever you want, Fanny.'

He held her gaze for a second longer. She wished that she had not spoken so harshly but she could not bring herself to apologise. She watched him turn away and stride angrily towards his mare, mount it and ride off without turning back.

❖ CHAPTER NINE ❖

Evenings at *Rosewood* had become dull, lifeless affairs. Henry Blackburn would return from work and silently, morosely eat the meal laid on the table for him by his daughters, and then retire to his study to find solace in the estate bookwork. He expressed no outward interest in his offspring. The pain and loss that he was suffering, combined with an innate inability to share his feelings, imprisoned him, driving him further and further from the companionship of his family. *Rosewood* had become like a tomb since his beloved Maria's untimely death.

Richard had of late felt a musty sense of suffocation in his home. It left him unable to sleep. Each night became more restless than the last. His head whirred with confusion, with images of his lost mother, frightful visions of Amos Johnson stalking the old hotel, and pictures of Fanny, one moment a kindly, understanding teacher, the next a witch.

One night, when all at *Rosewood* were sleeping, he was overcome with an insurmountable desire to escape, to slip silently from his bed and run wildly from his home into the freedom of the night. How sweet and fragrant the night air smelled to him, leading him along his path with a carefree sense of exhilaration. Once clear of the house and its dark, creaking corridors, he ran wildly along the dusty path towards the village. He did not know why. He had not consciously chosen this direction.

He reached the village by the upper route and paused there an instant to gaze down on the tiny sleeping hamlet. Nothing seemed to move or breathe in the lonely, mountain goldmining town. Not one smoking chimney, as summer approached, gave evidence of life. After his moment's reflection he set off again, stumbling and hurrying down to the lower path, where he dodged in and out of the shadows of the few homesteads and stores that seemed to be leading him to the old hotel.

Once alongside the old building he paused again, breathless and high, uncertain what to do. He waited a few moments, pressed against the side wall of the neighbouring general store, listening. Not a sound emanated from the school. Still he stayed, regarding it, considering its powers, uncertain of its fascination, willing it to impart its secret to him.

Then, from the stillness, the silence, came a sound. A scuffling sound. It seemed to be at the rear of the building. He listened hard but was unable to make out what it was. Cautiously he stepped away from his shadowy corner and inched himself towards the side of the school verandah. He crept as steadily as a stalking cat. As he reached his destination he saw something, the shadow of something moving.

In the starlit darkness he could not make out the form of the shadow that lay, distorted, on the back wall of the building. He needed to move closer. He felt his heart begin to thump as he dropped down into a crouching position and sidled closer to the source of the sound. He knew the tiny window that he was crawling below must be Fanny's bedroom and that any sound from him might wake her. He passed beneath it carefully and then painstakingly stood up again. The last few steps he moved, cautiously as he was able, with his back to the wall so that he could peer around the corner to spy, unobserved, whatever was moving there, scuffling in the night.

He longed to turn his head around that dreadful corner, yet he feared what might reveal itself to him. As he inched the last tiny steps he doubted his own courage. Often he had conjured up this creature in his mind, this figure of a dead man. For he was certain that the ghost of Amos Johnson was moving close to him, beyond the wall. He could imagine its ugliness. He was uncertain if he had the courage to peer around that corner. Nothing stood between him and the revelation of what moved behind the building.

Fanny awoke feeling clammy and uncomfortable. Though she was not aware of it, precisely the same noise that had disturbed her sleep a few weeks before woke her again this night. Tossing restlessly in bed, she blamed herself for what Joseph would perceive as her vile ungratefulness. 'Why,' she asked herself, 'have I hurt the one person who cares for me?' Locked within her own concerns she sat up and groped to light the lamp, unaware of the movements outside.

Richard saw the tiny side window, which only seconds ago he had sidled under so cautiously, light up. He froze and pinned himself against the wall, conscious that the creature moving so close to him, yet out of sight, was probably unaware that any life had been disturbed within the building. Or worse! Perhaps that was the very purpose of the ghostly movements. Perhaps it was intending to wake Fanny, to frighten her, even to kill her!

Fanny, fully awake now, was becoming aware of movement outside the building. 'That must be what woke me,' she thought. Although aware that it might be the same rustling, burrowing that had troubled her sleep last time, she dismissed it. It did not cause her any panic. Her mind was troubled another way, plagued as she was with her own wretched ungratefulness.

Richard heard Fanny moving inside her little room. 'She must be coming to the window! She can't fail to see me!' He was pinned to the wall less than five feet from the window. He saw the lamp begin to wave to and fro and dropped down to the ground. He lay close to the wall praying that if she did peer out she would only look from right to left. How his heart palpitated! 'Please don't let her look down,' he prayed.

Fanny had indeed picked up her lamp and carried it, not to the window, but to a small writing desk. She had decided to write Joseph a note, a few simple words of apology.

Richard lay waiting for the window to open. He calculated the length of time it would take her to cross the tiny room. Still it remained shut. And the swaying lamp became still. 'She must have changed her mind.'

He knew now was the moment to make his lucky escape. With the muted scuffling still sounding in his ears he crawled like a snake across the dusty ground. His destination was the general store. If he could reach there unobserved he would be safe. He could then hurry along behind the homestead and climb to the upper path, securing his flight home.

Fanny threw her pen onto the paper. What was there to say? How could she blame herself when she had spoken her honest mind? Had she not maintained the standards of any decent young woman? It was he, Joseph, who had spoken out of place. Had she not stopped him he would have declared love to her! Surely her gratitude to him was no basis for opening the way for such intimate conversations? It was he who must graciously understand her position. She had been correct.

Feeling more at peace with herself she made her way across the little room and turned down the lamp. As she lay her pretty head against the pillow, a tiny nagging voice asked her, 'Is it really only gratitude I feel?' Was she not also a little afraid of her feelings in Joseph's presence?

As Richard hurried along the starlit pathway he turned back to gaze down, once more, on the sleeping village. Once more nothing moved to disturb the silence of the night. His eyes wandered to the old hotel. Fanny's light was out. But suddenly, to his horror, as the moon came out from behind a cloud, he saw it – the figure moving against the back of the building! It was distant and shadowy. He could not discern the features from such a height but he knew for certain it was the figure of Amos Johnson. There indeed was the restless, murdered miner haunting the old hotel.

The ghost that all had spoken of but none, save him, had seen. It was real!

CHAPTER TEN

'No more dawdling. Finish your breakfast and get in the wagon.' The stern command echoed in Richard's ears. He threw down his napkin and stared at the table. He was almost too tired to eat anyway. His sleep had been restless after his return home. It had been close to dawn as he had crept, terrified, back upstairs to bed. His two sisters disappeared to the scullery to wash up and tidy away the crockery. After a moment or two he lethargically pushed back his chair, got up from the table and made his way through to the scullery. He walked to the back door, mumbling to the girls as he passed, unhooked his cap from a nail near the dresser, unlatched the door and passed into the yard.

He spied his father, a short way off, shouting orders to two young stableboys, not much older than himself, about hitching the horses to the wagon. Richard slumped against a tree stump. They would be a while yet. There seemed to be some problem with the horses' hooves. He stared blankly at four speckled chickens pecking at the ground, oblivious to the sheep dog incessantly barking close by. He didn't want to work today anyway. He had already decided he would visit Jeremiah but was at a loss as to how to escape.

And why had his father spoken that way at breakfast? They had all been sitting eating their food in silence. Richard's mind had been locked into the events of the previous night. He was longing to share with his father his secret fear that the schoolteacher must really be wicked because she was living safely in a place cursed by a ghost, but he couldn't admit that he had been there.

'Father?' he had said, picking at his damper.

'Mmm?'

'If someone saw the ghost at the old hotel would that prove Miss Crowe is wicked?'

'Someone saw the ghost! Who saw the ghost? Eat your breakfast.'

'But *if* someone saw it? S'pose Patrick had seen it? You said it's cursed, that's why we mustn't go there.'

'I don't want to discuss the ghost or the old hotel! I've got a lot to do today. No more dawdling! Finish your breakfast and get in the wagon!' And Henry had dismissed himself from the table, leaving his three offspring sitting alone with their meal.

'Richard!' Richard was aroused from his daydreaming by his father. He leapt to his feet and

139

ran across the yard to where three scruffy young labourers were sitting, in the back of the wagon, waiting for the journey to work.

'Get up into the wagon. We've wasted enough time!' his father commanded.

Why was his father so ill-tempered today? Richard could not tell. He obeyed without question and smiled shyly at the young men as he clambered up beside them. Henry shouted impatiently to the still barking dog who ran to the wagon and scuttled up, faithfully, beside his master.

'You'll have to take charge with the sheep this afternoon, Richard. I'll go to McCormack's. These damned horses need shoeing,' Henry called loudly over his shoulder as the wagon rolled out of the yard along its familiar way to the paddocks.

Liza Roundway carried her basket along the dry soil of Moogalloo's main street and made her way into the general store. She prided herself on her infrequent visits there, telling herself, and everyone else, that most of what she and her family needed she could provide for herself. She proudly boasted her home-grown produce.

'Good afternoon, Mr Burnley,' she said as she entered, not even glancing at Joshua Burnley. Her eyes prowled, assessing the assortment of goods on offer. Jars of sticky lollies stood close beside piled, ageing sacks of grain. A yellowing sign, curling at the corners and stuck to a wooden barrel, offered homemade lemonade for sale. Onions hung in bunches from the rafters amongst pots and pans, cheese stood in slabs on the counter, workman's tools leaned on the walls. Joshua certainly did a good trade.

In a darkened dusty corner Henry Blackburn was busily weighing flour and sugar into large brown bags.

'Oh, good afternoon, Mr Blackburn.' Liza's very words seemed to pounce. 'I didn't expect to see you 'ere. I would've, 'ad I seen the wagon waitin' outside.'

Unwillingly, he turned to face the woman he recognised by the familiar sound of her penetrating, inquiring voice. It was with a certain effort, not unnoticed by Joshua Burnley, that Henry addressed her, touching his large black hat as he did so.

'Good afternoon, Mrs Roundway,' he muttered begrudgingly, and returned hastily to the business of his bags. He was of the opinion that she expected to engage in conversation with him now that she gave her services at his home. It was offensive to him to speak to anyone not of his own choosing. Although he would never admit it to anyone, he quietly loathed this woman for her busybodying ways. However, he knew he must tolerate her or be forced to send to the city for domestic help. That would mean a servant who would live with his family – an idea that seemed even less agreeable.

'It's soap, I've come for,' Liza said to Joshua, closely observing Henry, discomforted by his coldness. She held her basket ready while the ponderous storekeeper proceeded to cut her a slab.

'I've 'eard tell that schoolmistress is flirtin' with the carpenter,' she announced triumphantly.

'What makes you think that, then?' Joshua asked, as he wrapped the roughly cut soap in brown paper. His question was spoken out of politeness. He was not greatly interested in the answer. Henry on the other hand, paused fracti n-ally. This information was something he knew nothing of.

'Young Patrick talked to my young 'uns. Foolishly tryin' to get 'em to school, is my reckonin'. Anyhow he said he thought 'is brother was sweet on 'er but she was just playing with 'im, invitin' 'im walking all the time.'

Henry folded his bags and made his way briskly to the counter. 'How much do I owe you there, Josh?'

'It'll be twenty-five shillings. If them bags is the five pounds you said you was 'aving.'

'The weight is accurate,' Henry returned coldly as he watched the bald-headed old fellow skilfully scrutinise the swollen bags.

'Right then, I'll trust yer, Mr Blackburn. I'll write it down on yer slate, eh?'

More than ready to leave these loathsome fools Henry nodded his agreement and walked to the door. At that very moment it was opened by Fanny. The two stood face to face in the doorway. For one brief instant, neither moved.

'Good afternoon, Mr Blackburn. I'm pleased to see you. I was thinking perhaps I might pay you a visit one evening this week?'

'I have nothing to discuss with you, Miss Crowe. You well know my thinking about your school. Please do not waste your time. Nor for that matter, mine.' With that he pushed his way ungraciously past her, leaving poor Fanny to face the two staring occupants of the cramped little store.

Liza glowered triumphantly at her. The slight she had felt at Henry not bidding her farewell was far outweighed by the delight she experienced at seeing Fanny thus belittled. Fanny made her way defiantly to the counter. Burnley, never one to involve himself in village gossip, had buried himself amongst his jars, pretending not to have observed the scene.

Outside, Henry placed the two large bags on the

verandah. 'No sense in wasting breath carrying them,' he thought. He walked hastily along the street the short distance to Joseph's, keen to reach his destination without encountering another soul. He held his head aloof and looked straight ahead. As he passed the old hotel he stiffened almost imperceptibly. It was rare for him to walk past the building. If business brought him to the village he used his wagon. This afternoon Blackburn had left the wagon with Joseph. Both horses needed shoeing, and he had decided to have the job done while he collected the provisions. Of course he would not have wasted his time explaining that to Liza Roundway.

He was thinking of the two incidents that had just occurred in the store. The information Liza had imparted and then the brief meeting with Fanny. He wondered if there was any truth in the story. He had reached no conclusion when he arrived at the carpenter's. The place seemed to be empty.

'Are you there, McCormack?' Blackburn called out, walking towards his wagon standing in the sunlight. The two horses, already rehitched, waited patiently, lazily swishing away flies with their long, dark tails.

Joseph was in the yard behind the smithy where he and Pat usually stabled recently shoed horses and where they housed their own bay. He recog-

nised Blackburn's Scottish accent. He put down
the bucket, brimming with creek water, for his
thirsty beast and walked around the side of the
smithy, past the blazing furnace of the brazier. He
saw Blackburn bending close by the neck of one
of his horses, scrutinising the new horseshoe.

'This seems to be suitable,' Blackburn announced
and moved round the front of the beast to check
the next hoof. Joseph, his skin stained and glistening with sweat, watched him. As Henry bent
towards the hoof he threw the blacksmith a surreptitious glance. He asked himself why the
schoolteacher, a woman who considered herself
well bred, would want to flirt with this brawny
fellow. It was the first time he had given a thought
to Fanny's attitudes or feelings. 'He's hardworking enough,' he thought, stooping to a hind hoof,
'but an ignorant, ill-educated fellow.' He dis-
regarded Liza's gossip as obvious nonsense. He
stood up, begrudgingly satisfied with the service,
and paid Joseph the requested sum. He felt it was
overpriced. He tipped his hat and stepped up into
his wagon.

'Come on,' he called to the beasts as he took up
the reins, turned the horses around and trotted
back towards the general store to collect his shopping. As he did so he saw Fanny walking towards
him with her full shopping basket, heading back
to the old hotel. Neither glanced in the other's

direction though both were all too well aware of the other's presence and what had just occurred between them.

'Ridiculous notion, her and McCormack,' Blackburn observed dismissively.

Richard paused a few moments to catch his breath and rest under the shade of a tree. Although the distance to Jeremiah's was no more than three miles it was a steep climb. He had forgotten how steep! 'What luck,' he mused, 'that Father had to go to Moogalloo this afternoon.'

He had spent the whole morning planning his unnoticed escape and had finally decided that none of the labourers would notice his absence from the paddocks. Even if they did, they were certainly too afraid of Henry's temper to tell any tales. After his experience with the ghost the previous night and realising at breakfast that it would be impossible to tell his father, he was convinced that Jeremiah was the person to confide in. He did not relish, though, the idea of approaching the gnarled old man. Although he felt a new bond with him he still found him repulsive. 'But who else,' he asked himself, 'would understand about Amos Johnson?'

He continued to climb, panting as he stepped.

He hoped the old man would be kind enough to offer him a drink. He was cursing himself for not bringing something with him. 'Even if I did run off in a hurry, I could have thought about water.'

He spotted the ramshackle cabin hidden amongst the trees, sitting close to the brow of the hill. It was a well-disguised position for such a solitary abode, visited by no one. Richard paused to catch his breath again, before braving the last twenty yards. 'I hope the old codger's there, and not in a rotten temper.' Jeremiah was quite well known for his tempers and his foul mouth, particularly if he discovered anyone snooping around near his shack. The puffed boy sat for a moment on a broken tree stump, looking up at the shack. This was going to be his first official visit to the place.

Several times in the past he had crept up this way with Patrick, sometimes with others too. They used to sneak up to spy on Jeremiah and to see if they could catch him counting gold. It was one of the local tales that at night the old miner sat counting his gold by the moonlight when it glistened! No one had ever seen this and the boys had wanted to prove it for themselves. That was years ago now. In those days they had never gone too close for fear the old miser would shoot them for trespassing or snooping.

Now here he was, two years older, braving the

visit alone. He stood up and slowly started to climb the last few yards. He dearly wished Patrick were there now, at his side. His friend and his confidant. Every daring act of his life, until this day, had been in the company of his friend. 'Alas,' he thought, 'my friend no longer.'

Just at that very moment Jeremiah staggered out of his shack, carrying an old iron pot. Richard held back for a moment and hid behind a boulder. He felt a little unready for the encounter now that the dreaded moment had arrived. He peered cautiously from around the rock, watching the old fellow. 'He looks like a twisted, weatherbeaten old tree,' Richard chuckled to himself. 'He's a bit like a witch himself, walking about up there with that steaming black cooking pot.' The boy took a deep breath and stepped forward.

'Mr Jeremiah!' The old fellow did not answer, engrossed as he was with stirring his presumably disgusting concoction. Richard felt no desire to approach the old man unannounced. 'If I catch him by surprise, it'll make him angry.' He tried again, this time louder.

'Who's there?' the voice answered, gruff and suspicious.

'Richard Blackburn, sir.' He walked the last few steps and paused a man's length from Jeremiah.

'What are you doing 'ere?' the old boy asked, squinting his eyes to study the lad. 'This is private property. I shoot all nosey busybodies,' he said. But he did not hurry inside for his gun, merely placed his pot on the ground and massaged his back, trying to straighten himself – a gesture, Richard observed, common to old men.

'I came to talk to you about our discussion over on the other mountain.'

Jeremiah looked blank.

'Up near the creek, where we saw Miss Crowe,' Richard uttered. He was a little ashamed of the memory, knowing that Jeremiah had caught him spying.

'What about it?' the old fellow asked impatiently but he did not wait for an answer. He hurried inside the hut returning a few seconds later, not with a gun as Richard had suddenly feared, but an old tin dish and bent spoon.

'You're right about Fanny Crowe, Mr Johnson. I have proof.'

Richard watched the miner carelessly spooning out a plateful of stewed rabbit. It smelt terrible to the boy, although he usually enjoyed rabbit. The old man began greedily eating as he stood listening to the boy.

'Proof? What do you mean, proof?' he scoffed, spitting particles of his food.

Richard began to feel uncomfortable. He could not understand why, but his body grew clammy and fearful. Suddenly he did not want to tell his story to this disgusting old man. He longed to run away but he could see no way of retreating. The old man waited. Richard had no choice but to continue.

'I saw your brother, the ghost, walking by the school late last night, or rather early this morning.' As he spoke he was conscious of how ridiculous his words sounded. For the first time the old man stopped shovelling the stew into his mouth. He looked hard at Richard, who cringed, hating the scrutinising gaze. Jeremiah seemed to be thinking hard, oblivious to the rabbit juice creeping down his beard.

'You saw my brother, eh? And what might you've bin doin' at the old 'otel in the early hours?' The goldminer had lost interest in his food. He walked slowly towards the boy and stopped a foot in front of him. 'Snoopin'!' he spluttered. 'Spyin' again, I'll wager.' He waved the greasy spoon accusingly in Richard's frightened face.

'No, sir, that's not true. I couldn't sleep. I went for a walk and just . . . and just ended up there.'

'You're a little toad! Always sneakin' about in corners, minding everybody's business. Just like yer mother! She was the same. Got killed sneakin' about in property that 'ad nothin' to do with 'er.' Richard felt tears of anger well up inside him as Jeremiah's voice became louder, more threatening.

'That's not true about my mother.'

'Well, you listen to me, you 'orrible little boy. You remember what 'appened to 'er. A lesson for you. Take heed. Or you may find yourself in the same sorry way. Now, get outta here. And if I ever find yer snoopin' and nosin', I'll shoot you. Just like yer miserable father threatens me. Tables turned, eh?'

Richard turned on his heels, passionately regretting his foolish visit. As he ran, sliding and stumbling over tiny bush plants, down the hill, kicking the dust into his tear-stained face, he heard the old man still calling after him. He no longer heard words, only the angry tone of voice. He did not stop running until he arrived, heart palpitating, at the fork of the road. One way led home, to *Rosewood*, the other to Moogalloo. He paused there, deciding where to retreat to when he suddenly saw his father's wagon returning from his afternoon of business in Moogalloo. 'Oh no! He mustn't see me now!'

The boy slipped briskly into the bracken. He needed time to consider the events of the past twenty-four hours.

❖ *CHAPTER ELEVEN* ❖

'Miss Crowe, I shan't be able to do my writin' practice,' a worried looking redheaded pupil confessed.

'And why's that, Thomas?' Fanny asked, glancing up at him as she tidied away her books. She smiled briefly at the two rows of scruffy faces staring at her from their wooden bench seats. It had been a satisfying morning. Today, with Thomas and his brother arriving from Benningee, she had seven pupils. Patrick, little blonde shy Mary Rowe, the two Watkinson boys, Timmy Garrard – a spiky, awkward child who belonged to one of the goldmining families – and now Thomas and Barnaby.

She prayed it might be a sign that things were improving, that people were perhaps warming towards her, accepting her school and judging her less of an intruder. She had noticed they certainly stared less as she walked about the dusty village streets.

'I have to go to the city, Miss, with my parents and me brother.'

'Well that's all right, Thomas. You can practise in the cart, while you're travelling. I shall understand if the letters are a little wobbly,' she teased. 'It's better than no practice at all.'

The nine-year-old boy sat down, satisfied with his first morning of school and beaming because his parents' business would not hinder his alphabet practice.

'Now off you go, the lot of you! I shall see those who can, tomorrow. The rest as soon as possible.'

The seven children stood up. 'Good morning, Miss Crowe,' they chanted in unison.

She opened the door and the sun burst into the dark airless classroom. All the pupils filed past, politely mumbling their thank yous, while the teacher held open the door. She followed the last child onto the verandah. He was Barnaby, younger brother of Thomas and too shy to speak unless brutally encouraged.

'Goodbye, Barnaby. See you in two weeks.' The little boy charged across the street without answering and ran into his mother's waiting arms. Fanny waved to his parents who had just arrived to take their two young sons off to the big city.

'If I were rich I could start a boarding school. That would be the answer,' Fanny dreamed, as she watched the two boys set off with their parents on the bullock dray for Sydney. Her gaze wandered aimlessly towards the store. A couple unknown to her, probably newly arrived miners, stood with Joshua Burnley on the verandah, discussing the price of an old wooden rocking chair that she herself had noticed a few days earlier. She had wished at the time, when she had read the *For Sale* notice, that she could have afforded to buy it.

Standing behind the three adults she spotted Richard Blackburn. He was waving energetically to someone. She called out to him, pleased to see him and to have an opportunity to talk to him. She was still upset by their meeting at the gully. He did not hear her call but stepped off the verandah and walked hastily in another direction. Fanny, disappointed, turned and went back into the schoolroom to collect the discarded papers and remains of lessons strewn around the floor.

Patrick had been the first out of class. Although he enjoyed school most of the time, he was always relieved when the morning lessons were over and he could escape into the warm, fresh air. This day he ran so fast past the general store that he did not see Richard waiting for him there behind Joshua's customers.

'Patrick!' the boy waved and called out. 'Hey, Patrick. It's me.' The voice was instantly recognisable to the Irish boy and he wasted no time returning to greet his lost friend. Richard, seeing Patrick willingly return, stepped from the store verandah and walked shyly but hastily towards him. He looked tired and upset. The last two or three steps between them were taken awkwardly, although both were eager to be in one another's company again. Patrick noticed the change in his young friend.

'Hey, you all right?' He paused waiting for Richard to join him. The two sauntered together in the direction of the smithy.

'If you're not busy this afternoon I'd like to talk to you,' Richard suggested rather sheepishly, ignoring for the time being the enquiry about his health. That, he would save for later.

❖

Fanny finished her tidying and then changed from her sober, navy-blue dress, the one she frequently used for teaching, into a lighter, cooler pale-blue skirt and cream lace blouse. Once dressed again she began preparing her basket. She put into it her papers for marking, a blanket for sitting on, a tumbler for water and a small cake that had been given to her by Thomas's parents. A present for the new teacher. She had felt quite touched. 'Life is getting better here,' she confirmed to herself whilst wrapping the cake and tumbler into a napkin. She thought of the approaching yuletide, which reminded her she had not written to Aunt Alice. 'No letters today, though.'

As she tied on her sunbonnet there was a knock

at the door. It was Joseph. They had not seen one another since her rejection of him by the creek. There was just a moment's awkward silence between them before he spoke.

'You promised to teach me readin' and writin'. It's such a lovely afternoon I thought we could walk and sit somewhere for an hour or two. I could begin my lessons.'

'I thought I'd finished school for today,' she laughed, and ran to collect her basket, calling back to him at the door. 'You can help me eat my cake. I've just packed it. I'm already dressed for the outing. Well,' she said, returning to the door. 'Your first lesson. I hope you're as clever as your young brother.' And they set off together for their afternoon on the riverbank.

They strolled happily in the afternoon sunshine until they found a quiet shady spot. Joseph sat on the grass under a banksia bush laboriously writing and rewriting the numbers one to ten while Fanny marked her children's school papers. The drumming of the surrounding cicadas quite deafened them both. It was a sign that summer was here. Finally the heat of the early December day and the tedium of repeating the exercise overwhelmed the blacksmith. He threw his pencil down onto the grass and looked across to Fanny who remained engrossed in her work.

'That's enough for today, Fanny,' he smiled. 'I'm

ready for that piece of cake now.' Fanny laughed and leaned over to her picnic basket and unpacked the cake, still carefully wrapped in its napkin. 'Now, will you give me another lesson after today, or am I a lost cause?' he asked as she handed him some cake and he passed over his sheet of paper with rows of numbers scrawled on it. Fanny brushed the crumbs from her pretty skirt.

'Well, you haven't your brother's concentration, that's for sure, but as everybody needs more than one lesson, I shall have to continue with you. And you still aren't writing the number eight correctly,' she teased.

'I think you're set on always being tough with me, Fanny.' Joseph walked over to the stream and stooped to wash his hands. 'Where will you spend Christmas, Fanny? Here in Moogalloo, or where?'

'I have nowhere else to go, as well you know. But I don't mind. I'm happy here now.'

He turned to smile at her. She did indeed look happier, he thought, more at ease than he had seen her before.

'It would please me greatly if you'd spend the day with young Pat and me. Or will you tell me I'm being improper to offer?' She looked at him, slightly confused, uncertain if he was teasing her.

'I don't understand what you're saying,' she said haughtily, and ate a crumb of cake that she picked from her skirt.

'You're a difficult woman, Fanny. Try to stop me if you want but I'm goin' to say this anyway.' He sat down beside her on the grass. Unconsciously she shifted slightly away from him. 'You're too hoity toity, sometimes. Don't you see, Fanny, that your English manners are out of place here? You may not care for me, like I do for you . . .' Fanny turned to him trying to interrupt him. 'Let me speak,' he continued decisively. 'As I said, you may not care for me, that's somethin' different, but you run away because you're scared. Not because I ain't good enough, but because you're scared of your own feelings. Whatever they may be. So don't go tellin' me I'm behavin' badly when I speak my mind. That's all.'

Fanny started to fuss nervously with her papers, busily tidying them away. She would have preferred to leave but she knew she could not.

'Perhaps you're right. I don't know. Yes, I am a little afraid, so please, let's talk of something else.'

'Well, will you spend Christmas with me or not?'

'Yes, thank you, Joseph. That would be very nice,' she answered shyly.

'You're last again!' Patrick called out gleefully to Richard who was still struggling to the top of a neighbouring gum tree. Richard, incensed, grabbed the highest branch and heaved himself up onto it. He sat panting for a moment, leaning against the main body of the fine bluish tinged trunk. 'You're outa practice,' the sandy-haired Irish boy challenged. 'I might be stuck in that silly classroom all mornin' but I can still beat you. I'm still faster than you.'

'You picked the easiest tree, that's all!' Richard retorted, fending off the brag.

They both sat quietly for a moment enjoying the panoramic view across the valleys and mountains surrounding them. Quietly they dreamed of places they could only glimpse in the distance. Cities, far beyond their simple mountain existence, where lives were lived that neither could imagine.

'When I've finished my learnin' I'm goin' to Sydney, to work in the city,' Patrick declared proudly. 'Will you come, too?'

'Mebbe . . .' Richard replied, gazing out into the hot hazy distance. He turned to his friend perched high in the neighbouring tree. 'What's she like?'

'Ah, just like any teacher, I s'pose. Bit uppity. Makes us call her Miss Crowe all the time and stand up when she goes in and out of the classroom. If you really saw the ghost why didn't you go back there last night? I would've. If I believed in them. Bet you were too frightened.'

'I damn-well wasn't. I wanted you to come, that's all. Will you? Come with me tonight?'

Patrick laughed loudly, happily amused. 'There is no ghost! It's a silly idea!'

'Well, come anyway.'

'All right. It'll be an adventure.'

Richard knew he had been frightened. Last night had been as sleepless as many in his recent past but nothing would have dragged him to the school alone. Jeremiah might have been there, waiting for him. He felt safer now, in the company of his close friend. He looked forward to Patrick's company later too, when they would go in search of the ghost together.

❖ *CHAPTER TWELVE* ❖

Patrick was still panting from his sprint across the village when he crouched down beside Richard who was kneeling impatiently under a golden-headed black wattle tree growing close to the chapel wall.

'Where on earth've you bin?' the Blackburn boy asked his breathless friend in a passionate whisper, 'I've bin here for hours!'

'Had to wait for Joseph to go to bed.'

'Let's go,' Richard sulked. 'I hope we haven't damn-well missed him!'

Patrick giggled. 'Course we won't have missed him. He doesn't exist. There is no ghost!'

'Then why've you come?' Richard asked angrily. 'Come on. We'd better go before we wake old Dalton. I've found a good spot for us to hide.'

The two boys crept cautiously from under the bush and scurried, half-crouching, towards their destination. It was a dark, moonless night. All around them wooden homes and distant hillside mining tents lay quiet and still. Not a light burned in the village. As they drew near to the school they paused momentarily, watching to make sure it was safe to creep closer. Neither dared even whisper for fear they might wake someone. Richard nudged his friend and signalled to him to follow. He pointed to a cluster of rocks on the cliff behind the school. Furtively, Richard leading the way, they crept up through the bracken towards the large boulders that loomed over the school. They scrambled up onto the flattest rock and slid down behind its jagged rear side.

'We can see the whole building from here. That's where I saw him before. Just there.' Richard pointed to a spot, some twenty yards directly below them. It was close to the back wall of Fanny's bedroom. The two boys peered into the dark night and then slid back down behind the stone boulder, huddling together for warmth and comfort on a bed of fallen leaves and twigs.

An hour or so passed. Neither spoke. Both were feeling chilled and shivery from the misty mountain air. It had not occurred to either boy that a blanket would have given protection against the cold damp night. Even Richard, who was bravely playing the expert at these late-night vigils, had not considered the discomfort.

The moon appeared, milky and indistinct but sufficient to provide them with a source of light. They passed the first hours fairly contentedly, watching and spotting stars and silently naming them, and listening to the distant sounds of owls screeching, a sleepless dog barking, and a possum or two scurrying in the undergrowth.

Suddenly something rustled in the nearby leaves. The boys froze with terror. They sat even closer to one another in dread of discovering what was moving. A twig cracked loudly nearby. The sound of a heavy step on the earth moved closer. Even Patrick grew fearfully expectant. 'Blimey! It's Amos Johnson!' he mouthed. Both boys, excited and terrified, awaited the arrival of the dead miner. But nothing or no one appeared. Their heavy-footed nocturnal companion turned out to be a false alarm. 'Must have been a bear,' Richard rationalised disappointedly.

As the hours passed and the night drifted along nothing new occurred to capture the two boys' imaginations and so they gradually fell asleep on the ground.

It was quite another noise that woke them from their unexpected slumbers. It was the chirping and screeching of the early dawn chorus. The warm sun rose slowly above the distant hills and valleys greeting their soil-stained faces with a new, young day. The damp warm earth under their aching bodies smelled sweet and rich. Both looked about them uncomprehendingly, sleepily uncertain as to their whereabouts. With the dawning realisation of where they were and what had transpired they leapt to their feet, anxious to hurry home to their respective beds before their night's escapade could be discovered.

As they scrambled down the hill, stiff and sore, Patrick mocked his young friend and his own foolishness for joining him. 'I told you there's no ghost. I must've been crazy to listen to you.'

'How do you know? We fell asleep.'

'I hardly slept,' Patrick lied defensively. 'Anyway, we'd have been woken by his wailing. Jeremiah claims Amos wails in the night. I didn't hear any wailing.'

'He doesn't wail. I know that.'

And so the two untidy boys continued their bickering all the way to the crossroad where they separated and hurried off to their homes.

'I'm goin' to watch again tonight. Will you come?' Richard called back as he ran off. He was anxious. These days his father seemed to rise earlier than ever.

'You must be joking! I want some sleep. You can go ghost hunting alone!'

And with that Patrick ran, full speed, back towards his wooden house leaving his dejected friend to race his two-mile distance as fast as his tired, sticky body would carry him.

When he arrived at the door, Patrick decided not to bother going to bed. He crept quietly into the cramped kitchen, boiled some water in the billy on the stove, made some tea and had a wash. He knew if he went to sleep at this early hour he would never wake for school.

When Joseph got up he found his young brother waiting for him. 'You're up early,' he observed, surprised, and drank the strong black tea Patrick had prepared for him.

❖

Fanny, exasperated, slapped her text book against her desk with a resounding thud.

'Patrick! Will you please wake up! You have spent most of this morning's lessons asleep.'

The freckle-faced boy opened his eyes instantly, aware that someone was speaking to him. He also heard a great deal of giggling around him. Yes, there was a stern voice shouting at him.

'Patrick, I am speaking to you.'

The sleepy young man was quite suddenly very aware of where he was and who was shouting at him. At the front of the classroom stood Fanny, in her navy-blue dress, sternly clasping her book and staring crossly in his direction.

'Patrick, I am waiting. I will not ask again. And please stand up when I'm addressing you.' The poor boy rose to his feet. He had no idea what Miss Crowe was waiting for and he sensed this was

165

not the moment to ask her to repeat her question. He decided his best defence would be bluff.

'I'm sorry, Miss Crowe. I cannot . . .' But he drifted off, unable to think of any answer that might satisfy her.

'You cannot what, Patrick?' Once again the small class burst into peals of laughter. 'You cannot what, Patrick? And the rest of you, this is no laughing matter.' Alas, the other pupils were not to be silenced. Their only concession was sniggering, heads close to their desks.

'I cannot remember the answer,' Patrick continued weakly, aware that he was completely at a loss. 'I think I must have dozed off.' Once again the class erupted into howls of laughter.

'Patrick, I know you dozed off! I am asking you *why* you dozed off? In the middle of the history lesson!' The boy remained silent. Anything else would have made his situation worse. 'Sit down, Patrick.' Fanny sighed and continued reading an account of the Battle of Waterloo.

Every now and then Patrick saw her glowering at him. He did his best to keep his eyes open, and tried to look as if he were concentrating. It was a great effort. After a while Fanny lost interest in him. Finally the lesson was over and, to his utter relief, the class was dismissed. He hurried from the classroom as quickly as he dared, certain that Fanny would call him again.

As he made his escape through the village he saw Richard waving to him from the top pathway. He turned down the lane, avoiding a neighbour who looked as if she was about to speak to him. Up he scrambled, loosing his footing occasionally over stones and dry earth, until he reached the spot where his companion awaited him.

'What a morning I've had, Richard. You and your schemes!' He threw himself to the ground under the shade of a tree, where Richard was sitting lazily whittling a piece of wood.

Richard was silent, choosing his carving rather than conversation. He needed his friend's support. He dreadfully feared the rejection he would receive if he asked Pat to watch for the ghost again, but he did not want to wait for Amos Johnson alone. He *had* to persuade his friend to keep watch with him again that night. He felt certain the ghost would be there.

'Want to come fishing?' he asked. It was Patrick's favourite pastime and he knew it. 'Pa's gone to Benningee,' he continued, 'to sell some sheep. Won't be back 'til late. Thought we might sneak down to the pool at the Magongee Waterfalls.'

Patrick lifed his arms away from his head and sat up a little. It was a surprise to him that Richard made such a suggestion. The younger boy always waited for Pat's initiative. Anyway, he knew that Richard was not really allowed down at the falls

pool alone. His father considered it too dangerous. There was quite a current there.

'Sure,' the older boy said, rising to the challenge.
'I'll go home for my stuff. What about you?'

'I'll have to go back for it. I couldn't sneak it
out before. Father was still there, loading up the
dray. Didn't want him to know what I was planning. He's already furious 'cos I was so tired this
morning.'

'Don't worry. We can take Joseph's stuff. He's
gone off somewhere. Let's go before I fall asleep!'

It was quite a hike down to the waterfall pool.
They both knew it was really too late in the day
and too hot for such an expedition, but it was
downhill most of the way and the return journey
would be in the cool of the evening after a swim.
It took them the best part of two hours walking
through passes of black ash and scribbly gums.
For most of the trek Richard strode on ahead con-
templating how best to persuade his friend that
he needed his help. He was determined to enlist
Patrick's company for his night watch. His instinct
told him he *had* to be at the old hotel that night.
He could not explain his feelings but something
in his bones told him not to go there alone.

'There's no one here! We've got the place to ourselves!' Patrick shouted happily as he threw down
his fishing equipment. He was the first to reach
the pebbly bank. Richard arrived beside him

seconds later and dropped the sack onto the ground. He stared out into the vast, natural pool, sweat trickling down his face. The forest trees towering high above them and the distant sound of water falling dramatically into the pool cooled the summer air. He breathed deeply. He loved this spot with its lush earthy smell, brilliant green vegetation and dark, damp soil.

'I think I'll have a swim now,' Richard said. 'What about you?' He pulled off his clothes, grateful to get the sticky shirt away from his skin.

'Nah, I'll stay here. Prepare the bait.'

The younger boy dived into the cool, refreshing water. He was an excellent swimmer and found no difficulty making his way towards the middle of the pool. He paused to enjoy the dramatic panorama, paddling his feet in the deep water to keep afloat. Somehow during the afternoon, he had to persuade Patrick to accompany him again to the old hotel. He turned back towards the shore. His friend was already hurling the first line into the water. He saw Patrick beckoning to him to get out.

'Your line's ready! Get out before you frighten the fish away.'

Richard swam briskly to the water's edge, skimming elegantly through the water. He waded the last few feet to the bank, feeling the soft, clammy mud underfoot.

'Are you going to dawdle all afternoon, or are

you going to do some fishing?' The sound of Patrick's voice broke his train of thought, dismissed his sense of foreboding. He stepped lithely onto the bank and stooped for his shirt to rub himself dry. Patrick handed him his line. He took it idly and sat down beside his friend to await the first catch.

'Saw your brother earlier,' he told Patrick, 'going to the school.'

Patrick bit into an apple. He reached into their scruffy sack and handed another to his companion. 'So?' he said.

'Why is he always with her? Jeremiah says she's evil.'

'He's started learnin' readin'. She's not evil. Just bossy, that's all.' Patrick dismissed Richard's curiosity. He was little interested in his brother's attraction for Fanny. If the truth were known he found it rather boring. At this moment he did not much care for his teacher. She'd humiliated him in front of the whole class. He bit into his apple again, happy to have the lazy afternoon ahead of him.

'Listen, Pat, will you come with me again tonight?' I *know* there's a ghost and I *know* he'll be there tonight. I promise you.'

'Listen. You go. I don't want to sit all night again in the cold.'

Richard was silent again, considering how best

to persuade his unwilling friend.

'You've got a bite!' The two boys leapt to their feet. Their tiredness and the afternoon heat were both completely forgotten. 'Don't let her go!' Patrick shouted.

Richard felt unsure about bringing in the fish. It was a big one. But the commands being issued at his side forbade him to let the excited, silver creature escape. He pulled and released as defiantly as his arms would allow him. Finally after several minutes the catch was ashore.

'He's a big fella!' Patrick exclaimed proudly, as though the fish were his. Both boys stared at the gasping, slithering freshwater blackfish. 'Well done, mate!' Patrick slapped his young companion heartily on the back.

Richard released the line from the fish's mouth and lay the dying catch on the grass. He began setting up his line again. Patrick beamed at him and returned to his own line. 'Please come with me tonight, Pat. I am scared to go alone.'

CHAPTER THIRTEEN

'I said this was a waste of time! Here.'

Richard took the biscuit offered by his grumpy friend and huddled himself up in his blanket, relieved to have remembered to bring something to keep himself warm. Patrick had thought of the biscuits. 'To stave off the long night's hunger,' he had said earlier. And it had indeed been a long night.

'Thanks,' said Richard, as he bit morosely into the last biscuit.

Both boys were feeling miserable. Any sense of adventure they had felt three hours ago had slowly seeped away replaced now with boredom and stiff aching joints. The biscuits had been eaten and the night was getting colder.

'I hope this ain't another wasted night. Can't think why I agreed again,' Patrick moaned. Richard feared the same. He was considering suggesting they give up and go home.

'What was that?' Patrick said suddenly, hearing a rustling sound in the nearby bushes on the

172

upper path. They listened attentively. It seemed to be moving closer, shuffling towards them. 'I think it's going down the cliff, towards the old hotel. It's alive. I can hear it breathing,' Patrick whispered, looking rather horrified. Both boys held their breath. He was right. Something was shuffling closer, moving steadily down the hill, wheezing rhythmically as it did so.

Richard felt sick and panicky. He knew instinctively that he was about to see what he had been waiting for. All at once he wanted to run home to the safety of his warm bed. Both boys remained motionless, concentrating hard on the steadily approaching sound. It was nothing they could identify, no animal they recognised. They carefully lifted their heads above the rock and peered over. As it came closer they could just about make out a shape in the dim light. The silhouette looked almost human, dragging its way along the path below them, towards the old hotel.

'Oh no, look there!' Patrick moaned.

'Wh . . . wh . . . what is it?' asked Richard, forcing himself not to shut his eyes.

'Can't see properly. It's too misty. Looks like a ghost though!' They lifted themselves as silently as they could above the head of the boulder. The spectre shuffled down the hill and stopped at the back of the building.

'That's exactly the spot I saw Amos's ghost

before!' Richard whispered, rather too exuberantly. The two incredulous boys watched as the creature bent down and began to rummage on the ground.

'What's it doing?'

'I don't know,' answered Richard. 'I think he's burying something. I'm going closer to find out.'

'No!' Patrick pulled at Richard's arms to restrain him. They scuffled for a brief moment, both wanting to impose their will, until to their utter amazement the being began to disappear.

'Look! I think it's going into the ground!'

The boys stood stock still. They looked at each other for an instant, took a deep breath and began to inch forward. The closer they got, the more puzzled they became.

'It m-m-must be a ghost!' stammered Richard. 'It's disappeared into thin air!'

Inside her little room Fanny opened her eyes and then shut them very tight. There it was again! Something moving in the wall!

'Whatever it is, I don't want to see it!' It was the same scuffling sound she had heard before – one minute behind her, the next beneath her.

Fanny sat up and listened, hardly daring to breathe as she wiped her clammy hands on the sheet. She hoped that whatever it was would not come near her.

'I know it's alive! Please God, let it be just an

old animal . . .' She did not dare light the lamp. She did not even dare move, rigid with fear as she was. Something bumped the floor under her bed.

'Oh,' she moaned. 'It sounds so loud for an animal. And it's getting closer!' She pinched herself and prayed that she might be having a bad dream. Her heart was beating so fast she thought it would burst out of her body. Prickling with fear, she lifted her sticky hand to her chest and held it firmly against her white cotton nightdress willing herself to be calm.

Outside the two boys waited for the ghost to reappear.

'I think we should go closer,' Patrick decided finally. 'Slide down on your backside.' They both scrambled over the flat top of the rock, lowered themselves into the thick brush and began the slow uncomfortable journey down the cliffside on their bottoms. It was still twenty yards to the spot where they thought they had seen the ghost disappear, and Richard wanted to reach it as soon as he could. Impatiently he began moving faster. His curiosity made him careless. He caught his foot against a small rock which went hurtling down the hill and landed against the back wall of the building.

'You stupid fool! You'll wake her!'

Fanny heard the thud reverberate against the bedroom wall. She jumped up like a startled cat.

'That is definitely not an animal. Something is knocking against the wall. It's trying to get in!' Try as she might she could not force herself to get out of bed, even to prove there was nothing to be afraid of. Her entire body was shaking. This time she knew in her heart there was something to fear.

The noise of the falling stone had frightened someone else. Slowly, from the foundations of the building, the ghostly figure re-emerged. Both boys froze with terror when they saw its head move up out of the earth. There was no boulder for them to hide behind now. They could not run away. Instinctively they flattened their bodies against the ground, not daring to risk moving an inch. They could only hold on tightly to one another, or to any piece of shrubbery, and try not to slide or disturb anything else. They dared not attract the ghost's attention.

They were close enough now to see the shapeless figure properly as it reappeared. What they both saw was more amazing to them than any ghost. Even in his wildest dreams Richard had not expected such a thing. It was not Amos Johnson, dead and buried, walking in the night to avenge his own murder. Instead it was Jeremiah Johnson, his horrible, living, breathing brother.

The boys lay together watching the old codger gather up his goldminer's pickaxe and his ragged sack. They could see he was frightened by the speed of his actions. He bent down and hastily replaced some dislodged timbers, then he looked nervously about him and hurried off up the path. The revelation had come as such a shock that the boys were uncertain what to do.

'What on earth was he doing?'

'There's only one way to find out,' said Patrick, 'and that's to go down there and look.'

This idea did not appeal to Richard one tiny bit. 'Why don't we wait and ask him tomorrow. Explain that we saw him here.'

'Don't be ridiculous. Come on. We'll have to hurry. It'll be getting light soon.'

The boys crept down the hill towards the building, hoping that the commotion had not woken Fanny.

'Get down on all fours,' Patrick suggested, mouthing the words, not daring to whisper. Quiet as mice they made their way. Only a few steps more and they would know the mystery. Patrick signalled to Richard to slide his hand gently along the wooden base of the building. 'I think I saw him replace some planks,' he whispered. Hurriedly they slid their young, grubby hands to and fro but found nothing.

'Are we in the right spot?' Richard asked.

His friend nodded and put his fingers to his lips. 'Sssh!'

Richard knelt up. He suddenly felt fearful that Jeremiah would reappear.

Patrick tapped him on the shoulder, motioning

that they try again. This time they used both hands, pushing and prodding all the planks of the wall and the supports below the floor, believing that somewhere there must be an opening. 'There's got to be a loose one,' Patrick muttered crossly.

'Blast!'

'Sssh.'

Richard had caught the palm of his hand on a nail. It started to sting and felt damp. 'I think my hand's bleeding.' Impatiently Patrick took his companion's hand and spat on it. Then he signalled to his friend to continue the search. Time was running out.

What had they seen the old man do? Richard continued testing the timbers while Patrick grovelled around the dusty, wooden walkway.

'Perhaps I was wrong,' Patrick thought to himself. 'Perhaps it was here somewhere, not the back of the building.' He turned to look back up the hill, trying to picture again what he had seen Jeremiah doing. As he did so his foot dislodged a small rock that had been pressed against the base of the building. Gently he lifted it aside and there underneath he found what he had been looking for – a tiny iron loop attached to one of the walkway boards. He triumphantly gave the thumbs up sign and slid his finger into the iron ring.

'It's a trapdoor!'

Cautiously they lifted the narrow wooden door

away from the ground and looked inside.

'Jeez, it's hollow! Looks like a shaft or tunnel,' Patrick breathed, peering down into it. 'It's very narrow and very dark. Seems to go under the building.' He sat up and looked at Richard who had been trying to see over his friend's shoulder. 'You'll have to go in, Richard.'

'Why me?' Richard asked horrified.

'I'm too big.'

'Jeremiah got in!'

'Shut up. It'll be getting light soon. You'll have to hurry.'

The reluctant lad turned himself around and lowered his feet into the tunnel. Neither realised how deep it went. Richard found he had no footing and felt himself begin to slide.

'Help, I'm falling!' In his panic he grabbed at one of the planks of the well-trodden old walkway now above his head, but it began to crack and then give way. Within seconds all the timbers were splitting away. There was nothing Patrick could do to hold him. As the walkway collapsed, the school wall beside it began to fall, and he was forced to pull his own arms away from his friend who was rapidly disappearing. He was helpless, watching Richard become trapped under the building. He heard his young friend yelling for help. But it was too late. . .

Fanny had certainly not been sleeping. She had

been lying on her bed, frozen with terror. Whatever she had heard moving was no creature of the night – not in the ordinary sense, that is. She began to curse her foolishness. Why had she mocked the village when they whispered the name of the ghost? Jeremiah had promised her that one day she would be punished. He had threatened her with the ghost's revenge and she had laughed at him. Here it was. Here was her reward for mocking superstition. Was there nothing she could do to save herself? She could run for it! Indeed she must run for it. But suddenly it seemed too late. At the very moment of her decision the wall began to crumble.

'Just as it did with Maria Blackburn!' she wailed. The whole building was collapsing and she was going to be killed! And now the ghost was wailing! It sounded to her as if the entire building were echoing the wail. She leapt from her bed and ran screaming through the schoolroom and out onto the verandah.

'Help! Help! Ghost!' she screamed. In her panic she did not hear Patrick's cries for help. Nobody could hear Patrick. Fanny's continuous yelling and hysterical crying drowned all other sounds.

Within seconds lamps were lit in the tiny hamlet as sleepy folk began to leave their beds and hurry, in dishevelled nightshirts and boots or bedsocks, towards the old hotel. The first to arrive, running furiously the few yards between their homes, was Joseph. He grabbed Fanny and began to shake her violently.

'Stop it! Stop it!' he shouted at her brutally. She was not to be pacified. Finally, in desperation, as an excited crowd gathered about her, Joseph smacked her. The blow woke her from her shock. As her tears and sobs began to subside she calmed herself enough to begin telling what had happened.

'Ghost!' she wailed again. 'It . . . it tried to kill me!' she said, heaving breathlessly.

More partially clad villagers arrived on the scene. Babes in mothers' arms yelled, dogs barked, children screamed to know the news. The word 'ghost' passed like an electric current amongst them.

Patrick, realising he could no longer help his friend, came running from the rear of the building, yelling at the top of his voice. He was shocked, and desperate for their attention.

'Somebody listen to me! Richard Blackburn is buried under there!'

Immediately the news calmed Fanny. Her hysteria miraculously disappeared as the horror of the situation hit her. Most people hurried to the back of the building, while others, waiting anxiously to hear what had happened, took the opportunity to gossip. 'It's *her* fault!' 'I told you she was a witch.' 'The place really is haunted,' they muttered suspiciously.

'What the hell happened?' Joseph asked his

brother but ordered him to *Rosewood* before the
boy could tell his tale. Patrick ran for his life
towards the upper path. 'Get Blackburn to bring
you back in the wagon!' Joseph called to the boy,
as an afterthought.

Meanwhile, Jeremiah was puffing and wheezing his way up the hill. The steep path between
his shack and the village was a well-known, well-
trodden path for the old miner. However, his
increasing age and the dim early dawn light made
it impossible for him to climb the hill quickly. He
had just begun the steep second part of the ascent
when he was halted by the sounds of a woman
screaming hysterically in the village below. He
paused for a moment to catch his breath and
listen . . . In the distance he could hear people running, shouting, opening and shutting doors. It was
too early for such activity.

'What the hell's goin' on down there?' Curiosity
aroused, the tired old prospector reluctantly
decided to make his way back down the path and
see for himself what was happening. He trudged
laboriously down the hill a little way until he had
drawn close enough to hear snippets of conversation. Someone was shouting across the busy, dusty
square. 'The ghost has reappeared!' This puzzled
him. He sidled down the path to hear a little more.
He could not fathom what was happening. Then
another man shouted out: 'Richard Blackburn has

been killed! Murdered by the ghost! Just like his mother!'

Jeremiah's blood went cold. He began to panic. Whatever had happened? All that he was able to ascertain was that there had been an accident and the boy had been killed. His brother's revenge, indeed!

'Jeez. Another flamin' accident!' He felt sick. He could not decide what to do. He must think quickly. 'What was that damn boy doing there? Snooping again, confound him! I told him no good would come of his busybodying ways!' But try as he might to blame the inquisitive young boy, Jeremiah could not stop himself shaking. Then he realised he was still holding his empty sack and pick-axe! 'Suppose I'm seen? Suppose that blasted child saw me? Suppose he's told someone?' The panic was taking control. He could no longer think clearly. 'I've got to get away!'

And so the flustered old goldminer turned on his heels and puffed his way back up the mountain to his odious little shack to gather together a swag of his scruffy old clothes, some bread and water, and his precious, long-hoarded sack of gold. Then, as fast as his old body was able, he set off into the hills in search of a place to hide safely until all the fuss had died down.

'Perhaps I will never be able to return,' he thought sadly. And his heart ached for his precious hand-drawn map, buried, undiscovered, somewhere under the old hotel. 'Well, at least I've got my sack of gold,' he added, patting the heavy bag tenderly as he lugged it away into the secret safety of the unknown mountainside.

❖ CHAPTER FOURTEEN ❖

'What on earth do you want, knocking us up at this hour?' Blackburn shouted angrily from his bedroom window.

'It's Patrick McCormack, sir. There's been a bit of an accident.'

Blackburn sensed the danger at once. 'What do you mean, "bit of an accident"?'

'The old hotel wall has collapsed, sir, and Richard's trapped under it.' Patrick saw, even in the dim light, that for all the man's coldness and anger he was genuinely disturbed. He saw the fear on the man's face. Henry closed the window and disappeared. Downstairs, in the early dawn mist, Patrick stood shivering. His wait was brief. Blackburn was at the door within seconds. He looked pale with fright, ruffled and untidy from sleep.

'How bad is it?'

The two stood confronting one another.

'I'm not sure, sir. Joseph said to bring the wagon.' It was all the boy could say. The rest they would know soon enough.

Henry Blackburn leapt anxiously from his wagon as soon as they galloped in to the village and pushed himself through the crowd. He was looking haggard and dishevelled.

'Get outa my way!' he shouted at the onlookers. Most of those not engaged in clearing the rubble stepped tactfully aside. He saw Fanny standing alone, wrapped close in her shawl, her face ashen. 'This is all your damn fault!' he pointed accusingly. 'You're no better than a witch, just as I always said.'

The crowd turned to Fanny. She saw the lamp-lit faces glowering at her accusingly. Blackburn had spoken what was in all their hearts. She knew it was pointless to defend herself.

Joseph, who was organising the rescue, wheeled on Blackburn. 'I'll have none of your foul temper here, Blackburn. Your son's under there. Let's just do our best to save him.'

The two men glowered at one another. Both knew this was not the moment to express their contempt for one another. Fanny watched Henry begin miserably tearing at the timbers and stones as if each separate piece was responsible for the accident. In spite of his malicious remark she felt a wave of sympathy for him.

'I'm going down!' Joseph called out to the half-dozen men working as a rescue team. 'We've dug away all we can. If some of you keep an eye on

186

that boarding, stop it falling, I should be able to get down to him.'

Henry, like the others, followed Joseph's request without a murmur. Adam Roundway pushed forward, calling to another to give them a hand. 'This old walkway's completely rotten. Better make sure it don't start the wall caving in further.' Blackburn stood numbly pressed against the wall, staring down into the darkness of the tunnel.

'Is the kid still alive?' a voice in the crowd was heard to ask.

'Don't see how he could be,' was the downhearted reply given by Joshua Burnley. He had always quite liked the lad.

Patrick, who had been standing at the back of the crowd since jumping down from Blackburn's wagon, was still shaking with fear and tiredness from his long, cold night's vigil. He moved forward to Fanny's side. Both saw the desolate expression on Henry's tired face as he stood at the head of the trapdoor hoping for a miracle.

'If I could only do something,' Fanny whispered. She put her arm around Patrick's shoulder. It did appear to be hopeless. The crowd stood restless yet silent, occasionally exchanging a murmured comment. The early morning warmth began to creep around the back of the school building. Not a sound emanated from the tunnel. Minutes dragged past without a whisper of hope.

Then, all of a sudden, Joseph's muffled voice cried out: 'I can hear him!' Fanny looked to Blackburn. She alone saw the relief, the tears of relief flow down the face of the boy's lonely father. 'I'm bringing him up. Someone throw me down a couple of ropes and then get ready to take him from me,' Joseph shouted.

Within moments the boy's bloodied head began to emerge. Henry could do nothing. His hands and body were pressed against the wall, holding it in place lest there was the slightest danger of another section crumbling. Patrick moved quickly from Fanny's side, along with Dalton and one other, to lift the unconscious boy to safety.

'I'll need help to lever myself back up,' Joseph called as two brawny prospectors stepped forward from the crowd to lend a hand. They heaved on the thick rope attached to McCormack's waist. Seconds later, as the boy's body was being lowered to the ground several yards way, Joseph appeared, sweating and grimy.

Henry held out an arm to pull the carpenter the last few feet to safety. 'Thanks, McCormack.' The two men shook hands briefly.

Meanwhile Fanny had rushed forward and knelt at Richard's side. He lay unconscious on the ground. She called to one of the nearby onlookers to give her a blanket. The youngish, plain woman mistrustfully took the grey blanket from around her shoulders and begrudgingly handed it to the schoolteacher. Fanny folded it under the boy's head, then put her ear to his chest.

'He's still breathing but he's badly cut. I think we should try to move him. Someone ride to Benningee for the doctor. Let's take him through to my room and put him to bed.' She shed her shawl and rested it across the boy's chest. Liza Roundway stepped forward.

'Adam'll go to Benningee, if someone'll lend 'im a horse. Won't you, Adam?'

'Take mine,' interrupted Reverend Dalton.

Liza looked down to Fanny who was still kneeling at the boy's side.

'But as for you, this boy ain't goin' back in there. You've caused enough trouble. You're as cursed as the place!'

Fanny stood angrily to defend herself as all turned on her. Voices all around began to accuse her, shouting 'Witch!'

'It's true!' another shouted, 'You've brought all this on!'

Patrick sprang from his young friend's side. 'It's not true!' he yelled passionately. 'She's not a witch. There is no ghost. It's all lies! There is no ghost!'

'What would you know?' a voice accused. 'You and your brother are as bad as her.'

'Yeah. Goin' to that school!'

Patrick tried once more to pacify them. 'Please,

189

it's Jeremiah! Jeremiah made it all up. We saw him tonight. That's how Richard got trapped. He was following the old man. There's a cave or something down there.'

Uproar broke out within the small community. Some villagers screamed for the lynching of Jeremiah – 'He's cheated us, lied to us!'; others for the lynching of Fanny, the witch – 'Encouraged our young 'uns to follow 'er!' Momentarily the dying boy had been forgotten, except by Blackburn who had pushed himself through the crowd to be at his son's side.

'Get out of the way! Let the boy breathe,' he ordered the now hysterical crowd surrounding Richard. The people backed away, allowing Henry to lift the limp boy into his arms and carry him through to the school house. The villagers followed in a curious procession.

'I don't know much about medicine,' Fanny called back to him as she hurried on ahead. 'But my father was a doctor. Richard has been badly cut by the falling debris and I fear he's broken a leg.'

Outside on the verandah Joseph, his shirt torn and grimy with dust, did his best to pacify the onlookers. 'Listen, there's nothing we can do here now. I will go after Jeremiah. If we all go it will alert him, so go home to your beds. Get some sleep.'

He led Patrick inside, into the schoolroom and closed the main door. Through the window they saw the neighbours. Some were still angry, some peered nosily into the schoolroom, others debated the truth of what they had heard and seen. All were unwilling to return to their homes.

Quietly the strong Irish carpenter and blacksmith led his young shaken brother to the back of the classroom.

'What ever were you doing here?'

'We were waiting for the ghost. Richard suspected something. Told me he feared something awful was goin' to happen. I didn't believe him. I, I . . .' And the entire story poured out.

Joseph listened patiently while, shaking and tearful, Patrick spoke. When the tale was told he embraced the boy, holding him firmly for a moment in his strong arms.

'You've been a stupid fool, Pat. Riskin' lives. You both have. But there's nothing you can do here now. Go home and get some sleep. I'll go after the old crook.'

Patrick nodded. He was very tired and close to tears. As he crossed to the door he glanced briefly into the next room and saw Fanny leaning over his friend, bathing his bloodied head. Henry was sitting on the bed holding his son's hand. In the background Reverend Dalton stood quietly watching. Patrick opened the door and silently left the school. The noise outside rose as Patrick made his way across the street.

'How's Blackburn's boy?' they enquired. 'Safe, after bein' in that cursed place?'

'Fanny,' Joseph whispered as he reached the inner door. She looked up at him but continued dressing the wound. 'I'm going after Jeremiah, now. Can you manage here until the doctor arrives?' She nodded her assent and then returned her concentration to Richard.

Blackburn sat quietly on the bed. He had not even heard McCormack, lost as he was in his own sadness. He realised how close he was to losing his own son. He berated himself for the little time and patience he had shown the boy of late. He prayed that if the boy was spared he would find a way to make it up to him. His black hat sat resting on his knee.

'I can't tell for certain if anything is broken. We'll have to wait until the doctor arrives,' Fanny whispered as she moved to the fireplace to boil another kettle. 'He seems more comfortable now.'

Joseph rode most of the way to Jeremiah's shack. He galloped the bay up the mountainside relentlessly. The early morning sun was beating on his back as he approached the brow of the hill. Before he reached the summit he could see the place was deserted. The delapidated wooden door swung to and fro in an unexpected early morning breeze.

'Blast,' thought Joseph angrily. 'The old codger's got away.' Nevertheless he scouted about outside but found nothing more than the remains of earlier meals being consumed by the morning flies.

He walked to the shack door, hanging loose on its hinge, and peered inside. 'Aagh!' he thought, his stomach turning. The place smelt putrid. He lifted a rabbit skin, still drying on a stump close to the decaying wooden door, and examined it with disgust. He was wasting his time. There was nothing left. The old man had bolted, taking everything with him. He looked about for a final clue. Nothing. He dropped the rabbit skin and hurried frustratedly back to his horse, kicking a rusty tin mug as he went.

'The old crook must still be close at hand,' he told himself. 'I won't let him get away.'

Back in the schoolroom Richard moved his head restlessly from side to side, muttering inaudibly under his breath.

'He's recovering consciousness,' Fanny whispered.

'Thank God,' Blackburn replied faintly, more to the boy than anyone else.

'Let's hope that's the doctor,' said Fanny as she rose to answer a knock at the door.

As she moved, Blackburn touched her almost imperceptibly on the arm. 'Thank you for your help, Miss Crowe. I appreciate your kindness.'

They smiled awkwardly at one another and Fanny walked through the schoolroom to open the door. It was Liza Roundway, now dressed. The two women looked boldly at one another.

'What is it, Mrs Roundway?' Fanny asked curtly.

'Any sign of my husband with the doctor?'

'Not yet. Shouldn't be too much longer now.'

'I came about his daughters. Must be on their own, over at that big 'ouse.'

Fanny had entirely forgotten Vanessa and Clarissa. She supposed that Henry had too. 'Just a minute, please, Mrs Roundway.'

She left the door ajar and went back to the bedroom. 'Liza Roundway's here. She's concerned about the girls.'

'My God! I completely forgot them!' Henry got up hurriedly and went towards the schoolroom door. His loyalties were completely confused.

'Why don't I go?' old Reverend Dalton suggested helpfully. He picked up his hat and set off purposefully to join Liza at the door. As they strode quickly across the street Fanny peered out before shutting the door. She was looking for the doctor. Instead she saw several of the neighbours still hanging about. They burst into animated whispers at the sight of her. She hurried back inside. She heard voices asking if the boy was still alive. She turned to Henry. He looked completely exhausted, leaning, half-sitting, against a desk.

'Why don't you go home for a while, Mr Blackburn? I'll sit with Richard until the doctor arrives. He's sleeping peacefully enough now.'

He nodded bleakly. 'I'd better attend to my daughters.' But he made no move to go. 'Miss Crowe,' he suddenly began. 'I believe I owe you an apology.' He spoke so softly, without raising his eyes to her, that Fanny had difficulty hearing him. 'I was mistaken,' he continued. His throat and mouth were dry, Fanny observed. She could see he was wrestling with his feelings. 'There is no ghost, it seems, no curse either. I forbade the children to come here because . . .' his voice trailed off. He scratched at the makeshift wooden desk with his nails.

'Yes, Mr Blackburn?' Fanny encouraged gently.

'If Richard gets well again, please God he does, I want them all to come to school. If they would still be welcome.'

Fanny felt herself flush with pride. 'They have always been welcome, Mr Blackburn. To tell you the truth I have been teaching your daughters for several weeks now.' She saw the flash of anger cross his face and then disappear.

'Well, then, it's as well I approve.'

She thought she could even perceive the glimmer of a smile.

'Mr Blackburn, if there is anything else I can do, please, do ask me.'

There was a long silence between them.

195

'Miss Crowe, my children have needs that I cannot satisfy. I have realised tonight that I need a wife. Not for me. I know I can never replace Maria but I must start to think of the children. I cannot care for them properly. They need a mother. You have agreed to teach them, to be with them. I think they are fond of you and you are here all alone . . .' He stood silently for a moment.

Fanny was utterly astounded. This man who, until a few hours ago had seemed to hate her, was now standing in front of her proposing marriage to her. She could not think what was happening.

At that very moment the schoolroom door opened and Fanny's first pupil of the morning arrived.

'Please don't decide now,' said Henry, buttoning up his jacket. 'Tell me when you're ready.' With that he walked from the school, leaving Fanny alone with her pupil.

Mary Rowe made a move to sit at her desk.

'Have you come for school, Mary?' The little girl nodded. 'No, Mary. There won't be any school today. You can go home.'

The tiny blonde child ran happily from the classroom. 'Thanks, Miss,' she shouted, as she banged the door.

Fanny turned to go through to Richard, hoping the door bang had not disturbed him, when she heard a commotion in the street outside.

Voices were shouting abuse and stones were being thrown. She hurried over to the window and peered out. Jeremiah was being brought into the village by a man on horseback. It was not Joseph. She hurried out onto the verandah. The crowd gathering around Jeremiah was beginning to grow. 'String him up! The lying old fool,' someone shouted. Jeremiah's hands were tied to a rope that was attached to the unshaven rider's saddle. He was being dragged to the general store, followed by a jeering crowd.

At that moment three other men from the village rode up behind them, momentarily distracting the crowd's attention from the scared old miner.

'We found him. Trying to escape he was. Whole damn sack of gold he had! There never was no ghost! Made the whole damn thing up,' one of the riders shouted, inciting the already angry crowd. Everyone was shouting and jeering at the old man who stood cowering in the street.

'Where's Joseph?' Fanny thought as she ran from the verandah. 'For God's sake, stop it!' she cried to any who might listen.

Jeremiah stood in their midst, trembling with fear, as several of them began to push him and shove him between them.

'Please, please let him speak for himself!' Fanny shouted.

'What's it to you, teacher?'

At that moment Joseph arrived. He looked tired and unshaven too. Fanny called out to him. The crowd was getting more violent and Jeremiah was being brutally knocked amongst them.

'Joseph,' she shouted. 'Joseph, please stop them!'

Joseph rode through the mob and came face to face with the farmer who had Jeremiah tied to his rope. 'Let 'im be, Warton.' The rider loosened the rope. The villagers quietened down a little, aware of the force with which Joseph spoke. 'Let 'im speak,' the carpenter continued.

Jeremiah looked from one to another of the faces glowering with hatred. 'I meant no 'arm. 'e cheated me. Me own brother. Stole the lot, 'e did, one night. We'd been digging together for years. We found a map. There's fortunes buried near 'ere somewhere. We was in the hills, looking with the map. He stole it while I was sleeping and took off with our gold. I didn't mean to kill 'im. I rolled the stone down the 'ill to frighten 'im away so's I could take the gold back. It went through the back wall while 'e was sleepin'. Killed 'im, it did . . .' His desperate confession began to dry up as he saw the faces in the crowd watching him, disbelieving him.

'Place is full of gold,' said one.

'Years we kept away from the hotel, believing him,' said another.

'Cheated us all,' yet another added. 'We could've

all bin rich. If we'd had the map.' The strength of their hate was growing again. Fanny, watching them, could contain her anger no longer.

'What does it matter about the gold, or the years you never dared use the building? You were the ones too frightened to go in there. Now you turn on him. For your own cowardice and blind superstition. Nothing stopped you but your own fear. You can't hang him for your own stupidity.' She turned to Jeremiah, who was feeling a little less shaky and rather amazed that she, of all people, should take his side. 'And now, Jeremiah, I must ask, since no one else has thought of it, what about Maria Blackburn? Never mind the gold. What happened to her?'

There was a terrible silence in the village. It was true. No one had thought about Maria. Jeremiah wheeled around towards her in panic.

'That was an accident! I swear it! Just like last night. I'd been digging in the tunnels, looking for my map. She went near the place the next day. Nothing was secure inside. Must have been a timber loose, or it just come loose when she fell. Whole damn wall collapsed. Same with the boy.'

The crowd, although more subdued now, began to argue between themselves as to how to deal with him: 'Still think we should lynch him.' 'Where's the gold, that's what I wanna know.'

Fanny walked quietly away from them back

199

into the haven of what was now genuinely her own school. She sat down at her desk. She felt strangely empty. Her mood was disturbed by the feeble voice of Richard calling to her from the bedroom. She walked through to him and sat at his side.

'Are you feeling a little better? You've had quite a bump,' she said, caressing his forehead.

'We found out about the ghost.' The boy slurred the words rather clumsily.

'Yes, I know. Try to sleep. The doctor's on his way.'

'Jeremiah, I think it's him.'

'You are supposed to be resting,' she said softly.

'I heard you talking to my father.'

'Did you indeed?' Fanny was surprised. It had not occurred to her that their voices were audible.

'I thought you were evil too. Jeremiah said so. I'm sorry I was beastly.'

'Sssh, don't get upset. You must try to sleep now,' she whispered kindly. 'We'll talk about it later, when you're well again.' She smiled, stood up and walked to the door.

'Miss Crowe?'

'Yes?' she said, turning back to face him.

'If you do marry Father, what about Joseph?'

'Joseph?' she said, hardly containing her surprise.

'I've seen you lots of times together. Patrick says he wants to marry you.'

'You are talking nonsense. Go to sleep, young man.' She walked back to him once more and kissed him on the cheek. 'No more of this silly talk.'

As she went into the classroom she noticed now she felt better, quite elated and happy. She sat down quietly at her teacher's desk. It had been quite a night. The school that she had battled so hard to make work was now truly hers. Even the Blackburn children were to be her pupils. That felt like a real achievement. But what of Blackburn himself? 'When he comes to collect Richard, I shall explain to him that my heart lies with my school. I am sure he will understand.'

❖ EPILOGUE ❖

'Jeremiah! Jeremiah!' Fanny called out from her back room. 'It's time to leave for Benningee.'

'Yes, Miss Crowe.' The old prospector put down his new quill pen, left the accounts and shuffled out of the schoolroom. Fanny saw him through the open door, proudly polishing the new wagon seat with the sleeve of his smart, clean shirt. A passing miner waved to him. Jeremiah waved back. Fanny laughed to herself.

'What a change,' she thought. 'And he looks so clean!'

At that moment Joseph stepped up onto the verandah. He paused to pass a word or two with the new caretaker, Jeremiah.

'Fanny,' he called as he walked into the cool dark schoolroom. He was wearing his only suit. It was a surprise to Fanny. She had never seen him dressed so elegantly before. 'G'day, Fanny. I've decided no more work for today. If you'll allow me, I'll ride with you to Benningee.' He chuckled.

'Silly,' she laughed. 'Of course you can ride with me. Come on, into the wagon.'

'How are you getting on with old Jeremiah then, Fanny?' Joseph asked as they set off out of the village.

'Believe it or not, he's a very hard worker! And he's good at sums. I think he's looking forward to the new school, although he hasn't seen any of the building yet. Says he'd rather wait until it's finished.'

'And what about you, Fanny? Are you looking forward to living in Benningee?'

'I couldn't have dreamed of anything better,' she laughed enthusiastically. 'My very own boarding school, for the whole district. I can hardly believe it. It's what I've always wanted. I shall miss dear Moogalloo, though.'

They rode happily together in silence for a while, enjoying the afternoon breeze.

'And what about me, Fanny? Won't you miss me?'

'Dear Joseph, please don't ask again. I don't want to marry. And as for missing you,' she gently touched his arm with her gloved hand, 'I shall probably never be rid of you, visiting at the weekends,' she teased, and turned towards him smiling warmly. 'You showed me how to fight for what I want, Joseph. Without you I would have returned to Sydney. Jeremiah's gold has made my dream possible. How could you expect me to settle in Moogalloo now?'

Joseph pulled on the reins and the two black

horses halted the swaying wagon. 'But do you love me, Fanny?'

'Yes, I do. You know I do.' She laughed softly and turned her face to the beautiful hills surrounding them. She spotted two rainbow-coloured parrots fly overhead and land, screeching, on the branch of a nearby gum tree. 'I want my independence, though.'

Joseph watched her for a moment then lifted his hand to touch her on the chin. Drawing her face towards him he kissed her gently on the mouth. 'You're a stubborn independent spirit, my darling Fanny.'

❖

Fanny knocked boldly on the front door at *Rosewood*. It was opened a few moments later by Liza Roundway.

'Oh, Miss Crowe! 'ave you come to see young Richard?'

'Yes, I have. Is he sleeping?' she asked as she stepped into the now familiar, elegant hallway. She turned back to face Liza before making her way up the stairs. 'How is he?' she asked softly.

'The doctor was 'ere earlier. Says he'll be right as rain by the end o' January.'

'I should hope so,' Fanny teased as she stepped onto the stairs. 'Your young Tom's doing well in school. He's like a fish in a pond,' she added warmly.

Liza recommended her dusting. 'Aye, so 'e says. Says 'e wishes 'e'd started sooner. Well, there you are.'

The two women smiled briefly, uncertainly at one another and Fanny hurried up the stairs. She opened the door quietly and saw Richard looking at her, smiling expectantly.

'Were you watching through the window?' she enquired as she walked to the bedside, kissing him lightly on the cheek and drawing up a chair to sit at his side. 'Happy New Year,' she whispered softly.

'Why haven't you been to see me?' he asked.

'I came last Monday,' she protested, 'but you were sleeping. So I told your father not to disturb you. I've been to Sydney since then to buy material for new dresses, and some furniture for our wonderful new school.'

She noticed that he seemed to be in a little discomfort and leaned forward to plump up his pillows. 'Are you in pain?'

He shook his head, fearful she might leave him, and wiggled himself slightly higher up in the bed.

'Miss Crowe, will I ever be able to walk again? Father says I will but I don't believe him.'

'Richard, don't be silly! Of course you will. You have a broken leg, that's all. You'll be walking properly again very soon and racing Patrick to the top of every gum tree in Benningee, I expect!'

'Patrick came to see me yesterday. Says we're heroes!'

Fanny laughed at the pride with which the boy treasured this knowledge. 'I'm sure you are. You're certainly my hero. A very brave and very foolish one,' she said, mocking adult responsibility.

'Is it true that horrible old Jeremiah's going to Benningee too?'

'Yes, he is. He's going to be the caretaker and look after the school. So you'd better be polite to him. After all, he paid for it.'

'But why did he pay for it? I thought he was an old miser?'

Fanny laughed. 'Because he didn't want to go to prison. People were very angry with him for lying to them and cheating them, so when your father suggested that his punishment should be to give all his money to help build a new school he agreed immediately.'

'Did you ask him to work there?'

'Yes, I did. It seemed only fair and I think he's happy enough.'

'Tell me all about it! What's it like?' he asked eagerly.

She enjoyed his enthusiasm. 'Well it's not finished yet but it's going to be quite spacious. I will be able to teach about sixty pupils from all the surrounding areas. There will be two class-rooms and two dormitories for the children who

206

cannot return home every day. And I will have my very own sitting room. And,' she continued proudly, 'a young governess from Sydney is coming to teach there too!'

'Will I stay there?'

'Indeed you will.'

'And will I ever come back to see Father?'

'Of course, silly. You'll come home every weekend. So will Tom Roundway and several of the other pupils. But Patrick will stay with me because Joseph is going to visit Benningee at the weekends.'

She saw his eyes begin to droop a little.

'Do you want to go to sleep now, or shall I read to you?'

'Please read to me.'

Richard lifted the book from under the pillow and handed it to her. Fanny turned to the marked page and they read together quietly, sometimes pausing for conversation, until the evening dusk crept into the room. When Fanny finally closed the book and looked towards the young boy he was already sleeping. She sat close to the bed for a few moments watching him.

'Sixty pupils and a boarding school,' she thought proudly. 'Well, dear Aunt Alice, I have found my place after all.'

And she leaned over, kissed the sleeping boy on his forehead and stole silently from the room.

❖ About the Author ❖

Carol Drinkwater was born in London of a southern Irish mother and an English father. 'But,' she protests, 'I am definitely Irish. It was my father's family, however, with their tales of song and dance and English music-hall, who first gave me dreams of "going on the stage". I used to sit in empty darkened auditoriums every weekend and watch my father rehearse his spot, his routine, and promised myself that one day I would be an actress.'

Carol studied at drama school in London and spent several years working in the theatre before being offered the part of Helen Herriot in the ever-popular television series, *All Creatures Great and Small*.

Although her international reputation has been achieved as an actress, Carol is no newcomer to the craft of writing. She spent a year, whilst filming *All Creatures Great and Small* in Yorkshire, writing her own weekly column for a Dutch magazine. 'They bought a long piece I had written about a visit to China, then offered me the column. Mostly I wrote about my travels.'

The Haunted School is Carol's first novel. 'I fell so in love with Australia when I was there to film *Golden Pennies* that I was inspired to write a book with an Australian setting.' *The Haunted School* has been filmed for television and Carol plays the role of the English governess, Fanny Crowe, in the mini-series of the same name.

Carol lives and writes in a rambling Edwardian house overlooking the Mediterranean Sea. She is currently working on a story set in the South Pacific, and is about to marry 'a handsome French film producer I met in Sydney'.